DEAL OF DARKNESS

ORDER OF THE ELEMENTS: BOOK FOUR

EMMA L. ADAMS

PREFACE

The magically gifted have always lived among us.

After centuries of living in hiding, a group of mages banded together and created their own parallel world to the everyday one, a paradise designed as a home for the magically inclined. Mages, vampires, elves, shapeshifters and many others flocked there, and for centuries, they flourished, ruled over by the Council of the Elements.

Then, several decades ago, the spirit mages turned on their fellow Elements and slaughtered them. The resulting war brought an end to the old Council of the Elements and left the magical world in ruins.

Since then, it has remained fractured. Clans of shapeshifters, vampires, and others rule the cities, while the Court of the Dead dominates the areas even the bravest fear to tread. It may be a paradise no longer, but to many of the magically inclined, it's still home.

Welcome to the Parallel.

1

Being dead was overrated.

I tried to pick up the dice and my hands passed right through the table. "What's the point in having unlimited free time if I can't play D&D?"

"You could always be an NPC like me," said Dex, my fire sprite sidekick. "Or take over from Devon as DM."

"I can't even hold a pen, let alone design dungeons," I pointed out. "Anyway, my poor tiefling rogue is stuck on standby until I figure out how to pretend to be human again. I can't go home like this without traumatising the other players."

Most liches looked the same, blank masked figures wearing shadowy cloaks, and had limited ability to interact with the outside world. Their leader was the exception, mostly due to his status as a former spirit mage, and in theory, I was supposed to have the same talent as he did. While I'd learned how to conjure up an illusion of my old face on top of my new masked features, picking up a die had proven trickier to master.

"If you ask me, you've been cooped up for too long." Dex folded his arms across his chest, his semi-transparent humanoid form glowing the colour of flames.

"I've already been around the entire castle a million times," I pointed out.

I'd got to know the Death King's territory inside out since my confinement here, from the vast stone castle to the high fence that surrounded the area of the swampland he claimed as his domain. The liches didn't have a designated area in the castle, so I kept my bag of belongings in a corner of the Elemental Soldiers' break room, next to the TV and games consoles. There was no point in asking for my own room when I didn't need to sleep anyway, but I missed having my own space. Admittedly, I could easily float through walls and closed doors without the need for a key now. Didn't quite make up for not being able to roll my dice, of course, but I'd long since grown used to holding onto the small victories. Even being dead hadn't changed that.

"Not the castle," said Dex. "There's a whole world out there."

"Most of whom want me dead," I said. "Or more dead than I already am."

He snorted. "They can't see your face. You could dance the tango in front of them and they wouldn't know it was you."

True. From outward appearances, I was just another faceless lich. Even my *voice* no longer sounded like mine, unless I made a strong effort to echo my former self rather than sounding like I was speaking into an echoing tunnel while wearing one of those voice-changing Darth Vader masks. Sure, I could freely swoop around the city without being recognised—if, that is, I wanted to risk being mistaken for one of the liches who'd ditched their master to join Hawker, the lich who'd done the impossible and returned himself to life again. How he'd pulled that off, I had no idea, but I'd be lying if I didn't wish he'd share that information, even if it was almost certainly too good to be true.

When it came to spirit magic, everything came with a cost.

Ironically, up until recently, I'd believed myself to be one of the few living spirit mages, at least those who weren't hell bent on world domination. Then I'd found out more of them lived in hiding in Elysium, but before I'd been able to figure out what to do with that information, my mortal life had come to an end. Now I was, deceased, immortal, and bored out of my non-existent skull.

"All right, let's go for a flight," I relented. "Maybe a phantom will pick a fight with us, just for a change of pace."

Dex whooped, flying out of the room. I followed at a swift glide, still feeling that odd uncanny chill every time I looked down and saw nothing where I thought my feet ought to be. While I'd astral projected a few times as a living human, I'd always at least been able to see that my transparent form looked the same as my living body. Now, a sheer cloak covered me from head to toe, while a hood and mask filled the gaps where my face ought to be. Beneath was nothing more than an empty space, a void of nothingness to which whatever had remained of my consciousness was anchored.

Several other liches drifted around the castle grounds

those had been Devon's hands, which she'd only begun to gain full use of again, and she was a long way from being able to make cantrips at the rate she used to. Let alone deal with the potential paperwork which would land on her head when the Order realised she was still alive.

Guilt swarmed me at the thought. After all, if not for me, Devon would never have been there to begin with. Yet if I hadn't shown up when I had, we might not have got out of there in time to avoid both of us being killed.

"Yeah," she said. "Anyway, I put a sign up in the shop saying we were closed until further notice. The Order hasn't called me, either."

"Seriously?" I frowned. "You'd think they'd at least want to check to make sure I wasn't hiding in the house."

"They might think I'm dead, too," she said. "Or their meddling department might have all died in the attack. I know, I know, I shouldn't joke about it, but they walked straight into that massacre when they let Cobb out of jail. I can't figure out how they didn't see it coming. Hell, *I* should have seen it coming. Those people didn't have to die."

"He must have planned it well," I said. "None of us could have known he'd have friends in the upper room ready to pull the strings and let him out, much less that he'd try an open attack here on Earth."

I spoke more to reassure her than me. I knew the memories of the attack haunted her at night, and they would have appeared in my dreams, too, if I'd had them.

"What're you up to, then?" she asked. "Your illusion skills are getting better."

"Not much to do but practise," I said. "I'm not exactly ready to pay a visit to my mum."

Last I'd heard, she and her wife, Elise, were trying for a baby. Instead, she'd lost her only child, and I had yet to break the news. Dad lived up north and we only contacted each other about once a month, but sooner or later he'd want to know what had happened to me as well. My family and friends should have been able to mourn me and held a funeral, but with no body to bury, I'd be hard-pressed to explain the situation in a way which wouldn't traumatise them for life.

It seemed cruel of me to ignore my family for the rest of my life—if this existence could be called 'life'—and I wanted to see them when I'd got the hang of pulling together a decent illusion, but I hadn't a clue what I'd do about my new sibling. I hoped the kid didn't turn out to be a spirit mage, though nobody else in my family was magical at all, so the odds were decently high that they wouldn't be contacted by the Order like I had.

"Understandable," said Devon. "I doubt the Order has got in touch with them either."

"They'd better not." I'd done my damned hardest to keep my shit show of a work life away from my family, aware that my magical ties could put them in danger just by close proximity. That I'd ended up associating with people like Brant who played fast and loose with the magical laws had furthered my determination to keep them as far from the Parallel as possible.

Nevertheless, the Order was in for a reckoning. I didn't know how many of its members were aware that Birmingham's branch was currently under the control of a coalition of sympathisers with the spirit mages who'd started the war three decades ago, but more people than I'd ever expected had secretly opposed the Order's decree

2

The Death King spoke after a moment's pause. "If you're sure about going to meet with Hawker, you'll have to commit to the act."

"You mean pretending I want to join him?" I said. "I can do it."

"I'll give you until Monday to make sure you're absolutely certain," he said. "Then you'll attend his next gathering."

"I'm certain." The part of me that remembered being human would never have been so confident at pulling off the act, but it was all too easy to forget how it'd felt to have emotions and thoughts which had once dominated my life. After the calm coldness of death, I knew why the Death King often struck me as fearless, though I suspected that I was underestimating the risk of getting close to Hawker. But I didn't doubt for an instant that there was no other way for me to return to being human again. To do that, I'd have to play the part until I gained enough information to bring myself back to life and finish him off for good.

The Death King must have suspected I wasn't budging, because he changed the subject. "How's your illusion progressing? I notice you're wearing your human face more often."

"I keep forgetting to move my mouth when I talk," I said. "Which kind of freaks out Devon."

"I can imagine."

"Also, I still can't roll a die yet. Or hold an Xbox controller." The average lich didn't appear to have any hobbies except drifting around and looking creepy, but I was still close enough to my human life to long for what I'd once had. And in the emptiness of my current state, I clung to that longing to keep from losing myself entirely.

I wondered if the Death King had done the same when the memory of his mortal life had been fresh in his mind. Yet while most of our animosity had burned away after my death, it felt too personal a question to ask, in spite of the ties binding us together. After all, it'd been the Death King who'd bound my fading soul to an amulet, saving me from fading out of existence.

"It gets easier," he said, and I wasn't sure if he meant the act of pretending to be alive, or the acceptance of being dead.

"Guess so," I said. "I'm a long way from being able to go back to the Order, if that's ever a possibility again."

The Order had a hell of a lot to answer for. No memories of my former friendship with Greyson Beaumont had survived their purge, but the enemy's words were hard to forget.

"He knows the people who are going to take over the Order

spirit mage again, and he had every intention of claiming back the House of Spirit for his own.

If I had to go to him first to spur him into action? So be it.

"Hey, I'm not gonna stop you," said Devon. "It's not like the Order's clamouring to give you work."

"That'd be because they think you're dead," Dex supplied, flying up to join us. "They don't have official lich ambassadors."

"They probably used to before they cut the Death King loose," I pointed out.

The Order had already tried to orchestrate my death more than once. Some of them thought I was too dangerous to live, while those who supported Alban blamed me for his death. Now Cobb and his allies had taken over the local Order branch, I'd never be able to set foot in there again, dead or alive.

"Their loss," said Devon. "I know you're staying away from the Order, but are you going to visit home before you go on this espionage mission for the Death King?"

"I don't know." I averted my gaze, aware that my face probably wasn't cooperating with me again. "I need to see my family, but I don't want them to become targets. It's not like I can protect anyone from here."

On the other hand, if Hawker caught me spying on him and I wound up getting killed permanently, I knew I'd regret not saying goodbye.

"I think we should both go home," she said. "I can carve you a cantrip which'll make it easier for you to maintain the illusion."

"Thanks." I forced a smile. "Are you sure you can make a cantrip that complex?"

"My hands aren't up to a hundred percent, but they're getting there." She wiggled her fingers. "Should be fine to carve a cantrip or two so you can visit the family."

A tight sensation clamped around the spot where my chest used to be. "How am I even supposed to explain where I've been the last few weeks? I can hardly tell my mother that I'm an immortal ghost living in a fancy castle in a swamp."

"You can come up with a cover story," she said. "I bet you can."

"I'm all out of inspiration," I admitted. "I've spent too much time alone lately."

"Yeah, dead people don't make for good company," she said. "I mean the other dead people. You know what I mean."

"Course I do," I said, trying for a smile which probably looked like a robot attempting to pull a human face. "Isn't it D&D night soon?"

"Yes," said Devon. "Tomorrow. Whether you can pick a dice up or not, you're coming to play with us."

"Okay, but only if we warn the others," I said. "I don't want to cause a stir if I walk through the table or accidentally let my face fall off."

"You're getting better about not doing that now," said Dex. "You looked like a melting zombie at first."

"Awesome." Just what the rest of our group needed to see.

"Chill, Liv," said Devon. "I'll have your illusion cantrip done by then, no problem."

Despite my friends' support, my worries remained intact. When I'd come back from death, I'd effectively lost my identity in the process. I'd become a faceless lich,

"I'll try to do better," I said. "Any news, then?"

"We're having a baby," she said. "Elise is pregnant."

My hand gripped the phone so hard that the illusion of my body flickered and vanished, and the phone fell to the ground. I scrambled to pick it up again, dragging my illusion back into place.

"That—it's great news," I said weakly.

My tone sounded as fake as the illusion of my face, but I couldn't forget Cobb's words when he'd been warning me about the danger he'd pose to my family if I stood in his way. If he and his allies found out I was still alive, my sibling would be in danger, too.

"Isn't it?" Mum said. "We'll come and see you soon, sweetheart. Let us know when you're free."

"I will," I promised. "Um, anyway, tonight is D&D night, so I'd better get ready before everyone shows up."

"Talk soon!"

Mum hadn't sounded so cheerful since her wedding day, and I didn't remember much of that, either. At this rate, I'd miss yet another milestone. I sank onto the sofa, my head in my hands.

Devon looked over at me. "Good news?"

"I'm having a new sibling," I mumbled. "I'd better hope Hawker and his allies *don't* find out I'm still alive, but if the Order is still recruiting, then they might go after my sibling anyway. They wouldn't want to risk another potential spirit mage slipping under the radar."

Devon swore. "The Order won't stay this way forever. Once the other branches find out we're under the control of a despot, they'll step in and unseat Holland and his cronies. It's not like Hawker is here in person, and his allies on Earth aren't spirit mages."

"There weren't," I said, "but Hawker's lich allies are turning human again, one at a time. Who's to say he won't start sending them here next? This plan of his has been in the works for more than a decade."

Devon pursed her lips. "Speaking of which, I had a thought."

"Like what?" I said warily. Devon's thoughts ranged from the ingenious to the downright dangerous, and she'd had an awful lot of alone time lately.

"If you're going to be a spy," she said, "what if I did the same?"

Confusion set in, then the truth hit me. "You mean spy on the Order?"

"Yeah," she said. "I need to get rent money somehow, and they have no proof *I* was involved in any of the recent events. And as long as I don't let on that I've seen you alive, they won't know we're still in contact."

"Hell of a risk," I said. "Most of their staff members are still under the delusion that they're following the law and that we're dangerous criminals. Also, they might think you're dead, too."

"Half their staff is on leave after the explosion," she said. "I haven't been struck off the rota yet. Frankly, I'm surprised they haven't shown up here, so I'll just call and let them know I'm alive."

"Better do it when I'm not around."

"Of course," she said. "I'll do it next week when you're off infiltrating Hawker's ranks. Cobb himself won't be at the Order's place. He might have said they pardoned him, but most of them will remember his trial. I reckon he ran off with those cantrips and is hiding out in the Parallel."

"All right, but if you see any danger, get out."

game, when I caught up with the others at the entrance to the liches' lair.

A sudden flash of brightness dazzled my eyes, and it only dawned on me that it wasn't one of Devon's special effects when several living people tumbled out of the node and into the room. A pale woman with long dark hair wearing a crimson-lined cloak landed at a crouch in the middle of the gaming table. *Bria.*

I was pretty sure none of us had summoned an unwanted Fire Element. "What in hell are you doing?"

"Long story," Bria said breathlessly, hopping off the table next to a stupefied Trix.

Elsewhere in the room, a short black woman with a streak of pink in her hair disentangled herself from a tall white guy with straw-coloured hair and an easy grin, and the two Spirit Agents looked at their surroundings with mild confusion. Dex was next to appear, zipping over the gaming table. It didn't take a genius to figure out he'd been behind their sudden appearance.

I gave the fire sprite an accusing stare. "What the hell?"

"We were being chased!" said the fire sprite. "Had to make a quick getaway."

"Into my house?" said Devon. "Dex, that is *not* cool."

Bria shot the sprite a disgruntled look. "Dex, you never said the node landed in her house!"

There came another flash, and a large chicken landed on the table with an ear-splitting squawk. The bright red light in its eyes and the bloodstains around its beak told me plainly it was no normal animal. Oh, that was just bloody perfect.

"Are we fighting a vampire chicken now?" Trix said uncertainly.

"I'll get rid of the chicken," Ryan said, picking it up. The vampire chicken bit them, and they exploded into a series of curses as Bria struggled to suppress a laugh and failed entirely.

Stifling a groan, I glared at Dex. "Please don't tell me whoever was chasing you followed you into the house."

"No, I think we're good." He cleared his throat. "So… want to do battle with a vampire chicken now?"

"I think we should go," Carla said uncertainly.

"No!" Devon struggled out from behind the table, nearly knocking the gaming board over in the process. "Get out of my house. And I swear if whatever's chasing you shows up here, I'll shut you in a cantrip delivery box and send you to the Order."

Bria and the others sheepishly left the room. Really, I thought I deserved a medal for managing to hold onto my human disguise, all things considered.

Once they'd gone, Dex cleared his throat. "So, how are you getting on with being dead, Liv?"

I dropped the dice. "Thanks, Dex."

And to think I'd expected that *I'd* be the one who'd derail the night's game.

last time I'd tried to get in, I'd been given a magical shock for my trouble, but now I had no physical way to open the door at all, magical or otherwise. At least the shadow the citadel cast hid me from sight, but it didn't appear to have a knocker or doorbell.

A patch of shadow detached itself from the night as another lich floated over to me. "New, are you?"

That voice... sounded familiar. *"Harper?"*

The lich made a jerky movement. "You know my name? How?"

"I thought you were dead." I'd seen her die during the battle with the Death King's ex-Fire Element, I'd thought, but it seemed I wasn't the only one whose soul had been saved. "Are you working for the Death King?"

"If you're here for the same reason I am, we'll have to talk later."

"If I'm here..." She was a spy, too. "I think I am. How do I get through that door?"

"Like this." She reached up and her hand passed straight through the door as though it wasn't there.

At once, it swung open. Two liches peered out at us, their shadowy figures barely visible in the yawning darkness of the citadel's doorway.

"State your purpose," said one in a low, cold voice.

"We're here to join Hawker," Harper said. "I reckon you could use a couple more liches."

"Come on in," said the lich.

I found myself glad of Harper's company as I drifted through the door and into the citadel. A wide, dark room filled the space within, featuring nothing but a spiralling staircase leading up to a door above our heads. Several other liches drifted around, talking in low voices. If I'd still been human, I might well have recoiled in fear from the haunted feel of the place, but the cold emptiness inside matched my own state enough that it didn't bother me.

"Name?" said the lich who'd let us in.

"Harper," she responded.

"Viva," I said, opting to go with the fake name Devon and I had come up with, revived from an old D&D campaign. "Isn't Hawker here?"

"Not yet," said the lich, whose masculine voice echoed in the surrounding room. "We meet all prospective liches to test their loyalty before taking them to his side."

I should have guessed they wouldn't show me into Hawker's real hideout right away. Wherever *that* was, presumably even the Death King didn't know.

"I'm surprised the vampires let you use this place as a meeting spot," I remarked.

"They neither know nor care," he said. "The vampires don't conceive of us as a threat to them. In a way, they're right, for the time being."

"Because the Death King is your target." My pulse fluttered—or it would have, if I had one.

"And his allies," said the lich. "Why did you decide to leave him?"

Did he genuinely want to know, or was he testing my loyalties? Either way, I had my answer ready and waiting.

"Why else?" I lifted my head. "I want to live again. I want rid of this curse, and it's clear that joining Hawker is the only way to do that."

"Same here," Harper said.

"You'll find yourself in good company," said the lich. "However, you're unlikely to have the opportunity to regain your life unless Hawker himself judges you worthy to join his personal guard."

Should have figured there'd be a catch. "I'm surprised it's even possible. You'd think someone would have undone the curse on the House of Spirit sooner."

"Hawker will explain everything," said the lich. "Be patient. Some of us have been waiting a very long time."

No kidding. The curse had been in effect for over three decades and had affected every spirit mage who'd been unlucky enough to be born into the House of Spirit. Only those who belonged to families without a history of spirit magic had been spared, along with people like me, who'd learned magic independently.

"I bet," Harper said. "I only became a lich recently and I already want to turn back. Would that be a problem?"

"Not at all," said the lich. "We accept everyone. My master is looking to expand his Court."

"Court?" I said. "What's he calling it? Because the Court of the Dead is already taken."

"For now." He looked between us. "We ask you to make a couple of promises before joining our cause. The first is that you protect our secrets. The second is that you tell nobody of the locations of our meetings. Do you accept?"

"Yes," I said, and Harper echoed my response.

I was in. Now I had to keep up the act long enough to save my soul.

"In that case, come back here tomorrow at the same time," he said. "My master will be here to meet you."

That's it? It seemed Hawker did occasionally show his face in front of his people. Either he trusted all his potential allies not to turn on him and overpower him, or he thought he had nothing to fear from us. Maybe he didn't.

"I look forward to it," I said. It was only half a lie.

Harper and I left the citadel, drifting out into the night. She didn't wear an illusion of her face, but I found myself imagining the girl I'd met in the trials. She'd been secretive but desperate, willing to do anything to gain the top position as the Death King's Fire Element and save her brother in the process. Instead, her life had come to an abrupt end, and she was doing a damn brave thing in coming here and putting herself in jeopardy once again.

"Did the Death King send you to act as a spy, too?" I asked.

"Sure," she said. "You seem surprised."

"I thought I was the only one," I said. "But I guess it makes sense for him to send as many people as possible. Who saved you? After the battle, I mean?"

"The Spirit Agents," she said. "They offered to bind my soul to an amulet, and I said yes before I could question whether it was a good idea. I wasn't lying back then. Getting my life back is the main reason I'm going ahead with this."

"Same here." I ducked into the side street off the square leading back to the node. "Not that most people actually know I survived, including Hawker and his allies. He thinks he killed me personally."

"I won't tell them," she said. "I'm not a snitch."

"Good," I said. "Are the Spirit Agents still allied with the Death King, then?"

"Of course," she said. "According to Bria, anyway, and she knows them better than I do. I'm sorry about the contest. For deceiving you, I mean."

"Davies was threatening you, right?" I said. "He and

his allies from the House of Fire. They put you under pressure, so you had no choice but to cheat in the contest."

"Yeah," she murmured. "You know, I reckon they're still out there. Not Davies, of course, but the others."

"Was Bria in a similar position?" I asked. "Is that why she fought on our side in the end?"

"Yeah, kind of," she said. "You'll have to ask to get her side of the story, but she's not the enemy. Nor am I."

"I hope not," I said. "Because given what we saw in there, there are quite enough of those around."

Worse, as long as Hawker held the only way to undo the curse, the Death King's people would keep flocking to his side. And for all I knew, he'd be aware of who I really was from the instant he set eyes on me.

After passing through the node, we floated back through the gates into the castle. The Elemental Soldiers would be asleep at this time, including Bria, who didn't know I was a lich. To be honest, I'd prefer to keep it that way. The Death King might have entrusted her with the position of his personal Fire Element, but that didn't mean I trusted her with my own secrets, including my new position as a spy.

The Death King waited alone in the hall, standing atop the dais as though he'd been waiting here for us to come back.

"No trouble?" he asked.

"Aside from the surprise of running into Harper on the way to the citadel?" I said. "It'd have been nice if you'd told me she'd be joining me."

"I wasn't the one who bound her soul."

"No, she told me it was the Spirit Agents," I said. "You

sent her in as a spy, though? And there I thought you were giving me a special job."

"I did tell you my last spy was killed, didn't I?" he said. "Besides, Harper volunteered. She was turned into a lich recently enough that she doesn't know if it's what she wants long-term. I wanted to give her a way out, if she so desires."

My mouth parted. "You mean she wants to die? For real?"

"If the option of turning back isn't what it seems?" he said. "Maybe. It's her choice."

"Damn." I'd never considered the possibility. I was just glad I'd survived at all. But to some, the idea of existing in this eternal half-dead form might be too much to bear. "Is that common?"

"More than you think," he said. "That's why I don't begrudge the other liches for trying to find a way out."

"Can't you—" I broke off. "The lich I spoke to seemed to regret turning his back on you, but he felt it was the only way he could return to life. Isn't there anything you can do to convince them to stay? Tell them Hawker's lying to them and he isn't what he seems."

"They already saw proof that he did the impossible and returned to life." His voice was clipped. "There's nothing more I can do to convince them otherwise."

I sensed it would be no use arguing with him on that point, so I let it slide. "What's going on with the other Houses of the Elements? Harper mentioned that she didn't think Davies's allies were all gone."

"That," he said, "is Bria's job. She's keeping an eye on the Houses, but Hawker is our main concern, since he's openly building his forces."

"By recruiting from among the liches," I said. "And I guess he has people in the Order, too. I know it's risky, but I could speak to the other liches…"

"The important thing is that you don't blow your cover," he said. "No matter what you might see."

"I'll reserve judgement on that until I see Hawker face to face." If he tried to kill someone, for instance, I might not be able to refrain from ripping out his newly regenerated soul.

"Olivia." He made a noise that sounded like a sigh. "You do enjoy testing me, don't you?"

"I'm not enjoying any of this, Death King." Yet despite the disconnect from my human emotions, the drive for answers remained, undeterred, along with the desire to make Hawker pay for what he'd done.

"I imagine not," he said.

I just couldn't stand to watch the liches turn their backs on someone who'd done his level best to protect them. Had the Death King truly done something heinous enough to deserve their hatred, or were they taking out their anger at the Order's punishment on him?

"Do they really think you betrayed them?" I asked. "The other liches, I mean? Hawker does, but that guy has a screw loose."

His expression shuttered. "I imagine the answer is obvious from what you've observed, Olivia. I'll see you tomorrow."

He floated through the side door and left me alone in the hall.

5

I walked down the corridor of the academy, my hands in my pockets. The pastel-coloured walls held an oddly unreal quality, while the flickering lights brought the nauseating image of blood splattered against metallic-coloured walls and floor.

I halted when I came within sight of a figure standing at the end of the corridor, leaning against the wall with his arms folded across his chest. His dark hair curled over his pale forehead, while his expression seemed conflicted.

What was his name? Greyson, right? I was forgetting everyone's names lately. He looked at me like he recognised me, but not in the smirking self-satisfied manner in which I'd been approached countless times since my trial. He extended a hand, revealing a cantrip.

"What's that for?" I asked.

"It's to help your memory," he said in a low voice. "It's unfair for them to force you to retake the exams without it."

Maybe it was, but using a spell before an exam would get me disqualified for cheating. "No, but thanks."

He withdrew his hand, his mouth pressed together as though suppressing some emotion. "Okay. If you change your mind, just ask me."

I watched for a moment as he pushed off from the wall and disappeared down the corridor. Weird of him to offer to help me. I didn't know him.

But I did.

My eyes opened. Or they would have done, if I'd been alive. As a lich, I didn't need to sleep. I could enter a kind of meditative state if I wanted to, but this was the first time I'd managed to successfully disconnect long enough to dream.

That hadn't been a dream, though. It'd been a memory. Lord Blackbourne had once implied my memories returned during near-death moments, though I supposed being a lich was technically a constant state of near-death. Or post-death. Whichever.

Either way... I'd seen my past. Strange how much I'd forgotten, even from the weeks after my memory had already been tampered with. How had it taken me until now to recall that I'd talked to Greyson at least once after losing my memories? In fairness, I hadn't known who he was at the time, much less our shared history. Back then, he must have known I didn't remember him. Yet he'd tried to help me.

That ought to prove I hadn't done anything that bad... right? Then again, back in those days, I was nothing more than an empty shell. Even with my magic theoretically intact and Dirk Alban dead at my hands, I was utterly harmless.

But not, it turned out, to the Order. In the end, they'd always planned to be rid of me. It gave me little satisfaction to know someone else had got there first.

I looked around the darkened room, a hollow feeling in my chest where my heart should have been. Then I filed the memory away in the shallow box of everything I'd recalled over the last ten years and drifted out of the break room, through the corridor and the back door of the castle. Lich or not, I had freedom at night I didn't have during the day, so I approached the node and astral projected, sending my transparent form through the light.

The world on the other side looked the same as always. Grey skies, terraced houses, and traffic. A total contrast to the wasteland of the Parallel, unaffected by the war. Only the Order remained, a tenuous link between the two, yet the people in charge might well bring a war here anyway. We'd lived apart for too long to close the gulf between our worlds without needless suffering unleashed upon the unsuspecting public.

I'd wondered if I might find the Death King here, but there was no sign of him. I didn't know why I'd expected to, or why it mattered. It wasn't like I never saw him in the castle anyway. My gaze landed on the squat brick shape of the Order's headquarters, and the lights still on in the windows. As tempting as it might be to do some snooping, it wasn't worth the risk.

Instead, I watched the sun rise over the rooftops then went back to the castle to look for my friends.

———

I didn't have to wait long. Ryan was up at the crack of dawn as usual, jogging around the castle's perimeter. They turned my way when I floated behind them. "Liv?"

"Of course," I said, slightly put out that they still didn't recognise me. Even if I did look like a faceless monster. "Should I start singing whenever I enter a room?"

"Please don't." They picked up the pace and rounded a corner.

That almost got a grin out of me. "Devon told you I can't sing, did she?"

"No, that was Trix." They halted at the castle's back entrance. "Trix said the one time you tried to play a bard, everyone hid under the table."

"Thanks for that one, Trix," I muttered. "I saw you two showed up for D&D night together. Did you meet up before coming to our house?"

Their face flushed. "He was teaching me how to build my character backstory."

"Just wondered." I'd seen them show signs of interest in one another, but I'd assumed Trix exclusively dated elves, though he wasn't typical of his kind. The fact that he hung out with a bunch of humans all the time was proof of that. Ryan, though, was his polar opposite in almost every way, from their serious manner to their tendency to strike first and ask questions later. While they'd begun to relax around the rest of us after joining our D&D group, I hadn't known they'd grown so close to Trix.

"We were helping Bria with a mission," they said. "We got talking."

"I guess I wasn't paying attention." I'd only been dead for a few weeks and everyone was already moving on without me. Or so it seemed. My own love life was downright depressing. I hadn't even seen Brant since I'd died, and while it was tempting to blame the lack of emotion whenever I thought of him on being a lich, maybe that wasn't all there was to it.

Maybe I'd buried what we had along with the life I'd left behind.

Ryan walked to the back door and entered the castle, while I floated behind them down the corridor to the Elemental Soldiers' training room. "You're just gonna follow me around while I work out?"

"I can spot you." My hand passed right through the weight rack. "I need to get in my practise at being human."

"You managed to hold it together at D&D night even when Bria crashed into the room," they reminded me.

"What in the world is going on with her?" I hovered above the mat while Ryan lifted weights. "Why did she show up in my house with a couple of spirit mages? And a vampire chicken, too."

"Haven't a clue, but I gather the Death King has been giving her secret missions."

"That figures," I said. "Your master is trying my patience, as usual."

"What's your problem with him?" Ryan grunted as they lowered the weights.

"The Death King?" I said. "He's being bloody obtuse, as usual, even though he has me risking my neck by spying for him. And then he has the nerve to lecture me about not blowing my cover."

They frowned. "And it's a bad thing that he's concerned about you?"

"I'm already dead," I pointed out. "Everyone else treats

me like a stranger. Except Devon, but she has her own crap going on. The whole world is scared of me, and the one person I thought would understand insists on acting like an arse. You'd think both of us being dead would have improved things."

"Maybe you both just push each other's buttons," they said. "I've never seen him act like he does around you."

"That's because I knew him before I lost my memories," I said. "There's a lot of important stuff buried in there, and he's the one person who might tell me the truth. Yet he hasn't."

"Tell you what?"

Right. I'd only told Devon about Lord Blackbourne's revelation about my involvement in Dirk Alban's death, since my untimely demise had overshadowed everything else.

"Allegedly, I *killed* my old mentor," I said. "With the Death King's help."

They put the weights down. "Seriously?"

"According to Lord Blackbourne," I said. "Can't say I have a clue how *he* knows. Even Cobb doesn't. He wasn't there."

"But the Death King was the only other witness?" they said. "Do you remember nothing at all?"

"I'm remembering pieces of it," I admitted. "But not enough. Lord Blackbourne thinks Dirk Alban told me his plans before he died and wants me to remember, but it's a little difficult when His Deathly Highness refuses to breathe a word about what really went down back then."

"The vampire lords think Hawker's using the exact same strategy as your old mentor did?" said Ryan.

"*I* think he is," I said. "He and Alban were allies, though

Hawker was hiding among the liches at the time. Cobb worked with him, too, but he lost his magic, so the Order let him stay in their ranks."

Their mouth pressed into a line. "Maybe there was manipulation in the Order from the start."

"Yes, which is why I need to check in with Devon," I said. "She's going back to the Order herself."

"To spy on them?"

"Kind of, but we—*she* needs the money," I said. "Turns out being dead doesn't pay rent. Who knew?"

"Ask my master for anything you need."

"You're welcome to try convincing Devon that," I said. "See, that's a prime example of what I'm talking about. It's like he's giving me an allowance on the condition that I don't ask him the wrong questions. I don't understand why he won't tell me his side of the story."

I did need to ask Devon about the Order, though. She'd been back there yesterday, so we needed to exchange updates on our respective espionage missions.

"Maybe you just need to ask the right question," said Ryan. "Or wait for him to be ready. He didn't expect you to survive the process when he turned you, you know. It shook him up pretty badly."

I stared at them, unsure how to respond. It was weird to imagine anything shaking up the Death King, though I was sure I'd seen him in a similar state in my last coherent memory before the Order had caught me, desperately trying to save my life. Between that and the new memory I'd relived last night, it painted a very different picture of our history than the vampire lord's claim that I'd manipulated Greyson into murdering my ex-mentor.

"I suppose Devon knows the risks, anyway," Ryan said.

"And she might learn something useful from the Order, assuming she doesn't get caught."

"I'm not exactly bringing in an income like this." I waved my transparent hands. "Besides, the Order thinks I'm dead. They don't have me pegged as a threat anymore. I'm the main reason they gave her unending crap over the last few years. Without me, they'll focus on a new target."

I hope.

Ryan picked up the weights again. "Tell her I said hi."

"Will do."

I left them to their workout and went outside, heading back to the node. Being a lich sure saved time getting ready, and within a few seconds, I'd crossed over into the living room of our old house. Hearing movement in the shop behind the door, I floated through and found Devon sitting at the desk, carving a cantrip.

"If it isn't our friendly neighbourhood lich," she said, without turning around.

"You can hear me?"

"The whole room just got a lot colder," she said. "Also, whenever you use the node, it messes up my aim." She held up the cantrip and showed me the crooked lines on the side of it.

"Sorry," I said. "Did you go to the Order yesterday?"

"Yeah," she said. "It's so *weird*. It looks exactly the same."

"It did right after the fire, too," I reminded her. "They're used to dealing with upheavals. Did you see Cobb at all?"

"Of course not," she said. "If Cobb's there, he's hiding, but I reckon he took off as soon as he had what he wanted. Holland, though, he's been promoted to a higher position in the upper room. I heard them talking about it."

I swore. "That figures. You know, I bet the identities of everyone in on this coup are in my missing memories."

"I hate to say it, Liv, but I think even more people are on his side than before," she said. "That, or Mr Holland did a convincing job of winning them over. Dozens of people are applying to be his assistant."

I pulled a face. Or tried to, anyway. "That'll be syco-phants like Judith French, I bet. Too intent on their own career progression to question whether they're taking orders from the right people."

"Too right," she said. "Anyway, there were no open mentions of spirit mages, or liches, or Hawker. I think most of the staff either don't know what's really going on or are too scared to stand up to them."

"So what did the Order have you do?" I asked. "Make them more cantrips?"

"I asked them to send any custom orders my way," she said. "They said they'd be in touch. And offered their condolences."

"I bet they did," I said. "Guess they didn't want to speak ill of the dead, huh."

Being dead to the people who'd hated me so intensely when I was still alive wasn't a bad thing. Especially Mr Holland, head interrogator and the person who'd tried to frame Brant and me for murder, among other things. I'd long assumed he'd been the person to order Cobb to be freed from jail, too. That the dick had made it to the Order's upper echelons came as no surprise. The universe was unfair in that way.

"Yeah," she said. "They haven't exactly set up a shrine in your memory, but we'll get there."

"Thanks for taking the risk," I added.

"And you?" she said. "How was your introduction to Hawker's people?"

"Weirdly straightforward." I ran through a summary of my encounter with Hawker's liches the previous evening. "Granted, I've yet to meet the man himself face to face. That's tonight."

"Good luck," she said. "I'll wait to hear from the Order. Unless you need any more cantrips?"

"I wouldn't say no to another illusion spell," I said. "So I can come back to see Mum and Elise."

"I can do that," she said. "No problem."

"Thanks." I drifted to her side. "Want me to help out here in the shop today? I don't have anything else to do until tonight."

"And do what, talk to the customers we don't have?"

An instant later, someone rapped on the door. "Think you spoke too soon there."

The door moved inward. I tensed, then relaxed when Trix walked in. "Looking good, Liv."

From anyone else, I'd have taken it as sarcasm. "Hey. Looking for Ryan?"

His face went brick red. "Why would I be?"

"I assume you're not here to buy a cantrip," said Devon.

"No... I came here to say Bria is very sorry for crashing our game last week," he said.

I frowned. "Since when were you carrying messages for her?"

"Since… um." He fidgeted. "Since Ryan and I were asked to help her with a mission."

"Okay." It was beyond me to tell what was going on with him at the best of times. Trix fitted the definition of 'absent-minded'. "That's a good thing. I think. As long as she's behaving herself."

"Anyway, I wanted to let you know," said Trix. "Do you need my help in here?"

"Only if you can conjure up a few dozen customers," said Devon. "Joking, joking. Just try not to scare off any customers who *do* show up. That clear?"

———

In the end, no customers showed up, but I got in a fair bit of practise using my lich reflexes as Trix threw dice for me to catch. I returned to the castle that evening to find the Death King hovering at the foot of the stone stairs in front of the doors. I shook off the question of whether he was waiting for me, though it'd been rare that I'd seen him outside the castle lately.

"Went home?" he asked.

"Just paid a visit to Devon," I told him. "She's spying on the Order, mostly because they're her only source of employment. They seem to be carrying on as normal, even though Holland got himself promoted to the upper room."

"Not a surprise," he responded. "They wanted as few people as possible to notice the disruption."

Not for the first time, I wondered if he'd always known about the planned coup. How much had I told him, before we'd gone to kill Dirk Alban? Maybe his current obtuseness was payback for my hiding crucial details from him back then. It was as good a guess as any.

"Some of it relies on wilful ignorance, I bet," I said. "People at the Order notice something's off, but they don't want to be the one to rock the boat by bringing it up."

"Exactly," he said. "I suspect, however, that the infiltrators are just getting started."

"They've been waiting for a long time," I added. "They have Dirk Alban's blueprints. I'm wondering when his name is going to come up."

"Soon, no doubt," he said. "However, I suspect he was better-known within the Order than outside of it. As for Hawker, he was here in the Parallel during Alban's attempted coup, as far as I know."

"Which is why the Order didn't catch him at it," I said. "Who exactly *was* Hawker, anyway? Because I don't know anything about him, not really. I'm curious about why he decided to wait until now to take the Order rather than joining in Dirk Alban's coup."

"He joined the liches before I was born, so I don't know all of his history," said the Death King. "He was involved in the team of spirit mages who started the war, certainly, but he kept his secrets close. I rather think he's more dangerous than Alban, in a way, and it wouldn't surprise me if he didn't join Alban's scheme because he suspected he might fail. Of course, that's guesswork on my part. Hawker did nothing to draw my suspicion while he lived here in the castle. He practised great patience."

"No kidding," I murmured. "Should I pretend to be a recently created lich, then? I'll probably have to, unless I want to make up a whole backstory, D&D style."

"Tell him I took pity on you and turned you into a lich

to spare your life," he said. "Also, try not to mention you're a spirit mage. Unless he tries drawing energy from you directly, he won't be able to tell. All liches can use the power of the nodes, after all."

"If he tries drawing energy from me directly, I'd be as good as dead anyway." Not a happy thought. Yet despite my misgivings, it had been a long time—since before my death, in fact—since the last time I'd felt genuine fear. Another perk to being a lich, I guessed.

The Death King made no reply. Perhaps he was recalling how Hawker had ripped out my soul, severing it from my body forever.

"Are you sure you don't know how he killed your last spy without access to their soul amulet?" I asked. "Because it seems to me that that would be useful information to have. It's not like I'm taking *my* soul amulet with me."

"I wish I knew," he said. "The nature of the magic he has laid his hands on is only one of his secrets."

"Lord Blackbourne seemed to think he was after whatever weapons started the first war," I said. "I promised to tell him if I remembered, and but it's more likely that I'll learn from Hawker instead."

"I doubt Hawker would tell you unless you gained his confidence," he said. "Lord Blackbourne ought to have known that when he made his request."

"Or maybe I'll coax him into letting it slip," I said. "You never know. I might turn out to be good at this stealth thing."

"I don't doubt your skills, but Hawker is older and more experienced than you are. He's on his second life, technically speaking. He won't let anything slip without intention."

"He's also willing to let liches from your castle join his cause," I pointed out. "That means he's opening himself up to a potential attack."

"I don't doubt he's prepared for that very scenario," he said. "Remember he's already killed one of my spies."

"Yeah, I remember."

I'd prepared the best I could. Now all I had to do was meet with Hawker face to face without ripping out *his* life force. As long as he protected himself, I had little chance of pulling that off anyway, so my best bet was to lie low and gain the information I needed before making a move. I needed to channel some of the patience that Hawker himself had used when he'd hidden in this very castle for nearly three decades, waiting for the right moment to strike.

Return to life. That's all that matters.

6

That evening, Harper and I travelled through the node into the centre of Arcadia, where the citadel towered over our heads. As a lich, I no longer felt the chill air of the night, nor the fear of a vampire leaping out of the shadows and biting me. Vampires weren't afraid of liches, and vice versa, resulting in a wary stalemate. Better than outright war, at least. I did spot a couple of revenants slinking around, but they fled at the first sight of me. A welcome change.

Harper and I entered the citadel via the front door. The dark room seemed to have more liches in it than last time, though the lack of lighting made it hard to tell. I'd guess there were at least twenty or so in there, none familiar to me.

As we moved through the crowd, someone cried out, an inhuman noise that echoed off the walls. I spun around, looking for the source. It didn't sound like a lich, that was for sure.

"Shit," said Harper. "I think a human got in."

Sure enough, several liches surrounded a figure near the door. As we watched, the darkness flickered, and the human's terrified face peered through a gap in the shadowy forms.

"Thought you could sneak in, did you?" said one of the liches.

"I didn't mean—" The man cut off in a guttural scream when the lich thrust a hand into his chest. At once, he fell to the ground, dead.

Damn. At least I wouldn't be caught out as human, though they might do worse if they found out my real purpose here. Then again, what was life, or death, without a little risk?

"Now that's out of the way," said the lich, turning on Harper and me, "come with me. You're the new ones, right?"

"That's us," said Harper, the merest tremble to her voice. "Where are we going?"

"Upstairs," said the lich. "Our leader awaits."

We climbed the spiralling staircase behind the leading lich. The door on the upper level opened into a large chamber filed with gleaming lights. I stared for a moment, surprised a room this big fit inside the citadel. Runes were carved into the walls, along with the emblem of the original Order of the Elements, which consisted of five symbols, each representing one element. The Death King had borrowed the design for his own—for reasons I had yet to figure out—adding a skull in the centre. The same emblem covered the walls and ceiling, while at the back of the circular room, an array of peculiar machinery seemed to be the source of the strange lights. Its white glow reminded me of a node, as did the buzz in the air emanating from a circular platform in front of the bank of machinery. Nobody else was in the room aside from our group of liches, and Hawker was nowhere to be seen.

"What's this place for?" I studied the machinery. It was sophisticated by Parallel standards, but I hadn't the faintest clue what any of it did. "I thought you said we were meeting the boss."

"We will take you to our base," said the lich. "This way."

Puzzled, I followed the lich to the raised platform, as did Harper. As we did so, another lich approached the bank of machinery and pressed a button on its surface. The lights brightened, and the humming intensified.

"What—" I broke off, and Harper swore quietly as more lights spun around our feet, surrounding the platform.

The other liches vanished from sight as the room disappeared. Energy surged within me as though I'd trodden on a node, and in another instant, we landed in a near-identical room to the first one.

What was that?

I reeled back, struggling to rein in the energy surging within me and hoping nobody had seen the way the light brightened around my hands. Unlike the first room, this one was packed with the shadowy forms of liches. Had there been a node underneath our feet the whole time?

"We're in another citadel," I breathed.

"Correct," said the lich. "The transporters in each citadel connect with one another, rather like nodes. That way, it's possible for us to hide our location from anyone who might come looking for our master."

I turned to him. "Does *every* citadel contain a similar transporter?"

"Yes," he said. "However, not all of them are in working order. This one was damaged in the conflict the other week, but we managed to fix it."

Damn. "We're not in Arcadia. So where—?"

"We're in Elysium," said the lich.

Good to know, if I wanted to make a run for it. I'd only been to Elysium once, when the Spirit Agents had taken me to their base, though the room itself was almost a mirror of Arcadia's citadel. The same bank of machinery filled the space at the back behind the platform at our feet. Groups of liches drifted around, along with a few humans. Spirit mages, I assumed. They were clearly allowed in, unlike that poor human who'd tried using a cantrip to disguise himself as a lich to get into Arcadia's citadel.

"What do we do now?" I asked. "Wait for the boss to show up?"

"Yes," said the lich. "I'll fetch the next group. What happens next depends on whether or not Hawker is in a good mood."

He drifted back to the raised platform, gesturing to another lich, who hit a button on the machine's surface. At once, our companion vanished in a flash of light. A chill raced down my back. "That thing doesn't seem to have a limit on how many people it can carry, does it?"

"Huh?" Harper said. "Why does it matter?"

"Well, it'd be convenient if someone wanted to gather an army from all over the Parallel."

She stared at me for an instant. "The Spirit Agents did that. That's how—"

"*That's* how they got to Arcadia so fast." Of course. It also explained why Bria had led them out of the citadel to join us in battle. They'd used the transporter as a shortcut. Which meant she'd already known about this place a while ago. Shouldn't really be a surprise, considering, but it gave me another array of questions to ask the Death King as well as another incentive to survive the night.

"Yeah," Harper murmured. "The Spirt Agents weren't the ones who set it up, but the enemy left their transporter turned on, so they used it to come to Arcadia and help out in the battle."

"Damn useful."

Transporters linking every citadel across the Parallel. The spirit mages had built the towers themselves, so it made sense that this was how they'd travelled around and consolidated their army during the war. Had the Death King made the connection? He must have. The guy was too smart not to have guessed. I had to wonder why he'd never come in here himself, but then again, he already had free run of the Parallel without the need for a fancy transporter.

"It can't be used to travel to Earth, can it?" I said.

"No, I don't think so," Harper said. "The transporters in each citadel link up with one another. There aren't any on Earth, I heard."

That made sense. The spirit mage armies had never arrived on Earth, but they'd decimated the Parallel in a short space of time. If they'd used the transporters, nobody would have been able to outrun them. Not even the other elemental mages. Was this common knowledge? Few mages talked about the details of the war, as there'd been such a large volume of casualties and the very foundations of the Parallel had shifted as a result. Brant almost certainly knew, though, since he'd been imprisoned in the

House of Fire, whose entire purpose was to punish mages for the crimes committed during the war.

I'd bet the Order had seen to it that the transporters had remained out of use, since after the war, the surviving mages had been left without any of their previous resources. And the House of Spirit had suffered the worst of all.

The platform lit up again and brought in another group of liches. I turned to Harper. "I'm going to do some snooping. I'll be back when our esteemed leader shows up."

I made my way through circular room, keeping a particularly close watch on the spirit mages, but none carried any visible cantrips nor any other signs to indicate whether they were former liches or not. Regardless, it came as a surprise to find that I wasn't afraid of them. Perhaps I ought to be, but a combination of being dead and the absolute shit show of the last few weeks had whittled my fear of my fellow spirit mages down to almost nothing. Even the prospect of seeing Hawker filled me with more anticipation than anything else.

A pair of spirit mages moved to intercept me. One was short and chubby, while the second towered over me even in my lich form.

"You're new," said the taller dude. "What do you think of this place?"

"I'm impressed with the setup here, but the refreshments leave much to be desired," I responded.

His friend smirked. "Yeah, they don't have many living people at these get-togethers."

"Yet," I added. "How quickly is he bringing people back to life?"

"Bit impatient, aren't you?" said the short dude.

"If you were stuck like this, you would be, too," I said. "Were you always alive?"

"Sure," said the taller guy. "Why?"

"What's in it for you, then?" I asked out of genuine curiosity. "I mean, if you're not hoping he'll bring you back to life, I assume there's something else on offer."

"You mean aside from our freedom?" said the shorter mage. "And being allowed to use the nodes without getting arrested by those stuck-up twats at the Order?"

"You think he's going to pull it off?" I didn't need to fake the scepticism in my tone. "The Order's pretty big. Global, even."

"So are we." The shorter mage indicated the machinery at the back of the room. "People here are from all over. We're from Elysium. What about you?"

"Arcadia," I lied. "So are you with the Spirit Agents? Or should that be 'were you'?"

Was anyone in this room from Earth? Probably not. Spirit mages hadn't been allowed to use their magic over on the other side of the nodes even before Hawker's coup. Still, they might've joined the Spirit Agents instead of coming here.

"Used to be," said the taller dude. "They had nothing to offer us, compared to Hawker, so we quit."

"Guess he did promise the world," I said, bitterness underlying my tone. "Hard to beat, that."

"Exactly," said his friend.

"You sure it isn't gonna end up like the last war?" I looked between them. "Because that didn't turn out too well for anyone. You might say the spirit mages came off worse."

"We survived," said the tall mage. "Like these citadels did. We're designed to endure, too."

"Most of you died," I said, growing more annoyed with the pair of them by the second. "Does Hawker have a plan that won't end in mass casualties like last time?"

"He has a plan," said the taller mage. "What's in it for you if you don't want to go to war, then?"

"I'm here to come back to life," I told them. "I'm not interested in war or power."

The shorter guy smirked. "You're going to be waiting a long time if that's your attitude. Everyone in here wants to be one of Hawker's chosen few."

I followed his gaze around the room, seeing the hundreds of liches gathering under an air of palpable anticipation. All of them were waiting, too. Sure, some of them might want to go to war for the hell of it, but desperation bred terrible decisions. I should know.

"Anything I can do to speed up my promotion?" I said. "Does His Highness require back rubs, or...?"

"Think you're funny, do you?" said the shorter mage. "Or are you hoping he'll make your death permanent?"

"I don't have a death wish," I told him. "Deader than dead wish, that is."

"I like her," said the tall dude. "Maybe she can catch his eye, who knows. He wants smart people, not just soldiers."

At that moment, I spotted another mage walking past... someone I recognised. Miles. He was the leader of the Spirit Agents, which meant he must be here for the same reason as me. Unless he'd turned traitor, but that seemed unlikely.

"I'll see if I can get the boss's attention, then," I said to the mages, taking the opportunity to extricate myself from the conversation. "See you around."

I tailed Miles across the room, not needing to try to keep my footsteps silent or my head down. He gave me a glance to acknowledge my presence, but he didn't speak until we came to a spot a safe distance away from eavesdroppers.

"I'm guessing I'm not the only spy?" he said in an undertone. "Nice costume."

"Not a costume."

"Oh," he said. "My condolences."

I gave a short nod to acknowledge his apparent genuineness. "Are many of your people in here? Because those guys I was just talking to seem to have ditched the Spirit Agents."

"We know they defected," he murmured. "Don't worry, we won't let them into our club anymore."

"Good," I said. "It's hard to tell friend from foe here."

"Generally speaking, if they don't say otherwise, assume everyone is a foe," he said. "I brought two allies with me. The rest are defectors."

"Aren't you worried they'll recognise you?"

"Not in the slightest." There was a hint of warning to his voice which indicated that part of him hoped they *would* recognise him. Damn if I didn't understand where he was coming from.

"Speaking of friends, mine has disappeared among our faceless companions," I said. "I'd better find her before the boss shows up."

The slight problem was that there was no way I could spot Harper from a distance when all the liches looked the same, and there were a good hundred liches in here by now. *Maybe splitting up was a mistake.*

Aside from the liches, there were maybe thirty or so spirit mages in the room, and not all of them had been liches first. Hawker was certainly being sparing with his new spell. But what had I expected, really? He knew what we wanted, and he'd hold the tantalising promise of a return to life over our heads for as long as possible. Maybe he never planned to turn us human again. Or even show his face…

I let that thought go as silence rippled through the crowd. All eyes turned to the front when the door opened, and Hawker walked into the room. His dark hair reached his chin, while his face showed a man in his early fifties at most. Not someone who'd already been dead for thirty years or more.

He looked directly at me. His gaze stripped me bare, as though I'd had a lucky roll on a camouflage spell to avoid an attack, only for the enemy to pinpoint my location anyway.

Oh, damn.

7

I looked away from Hawker's stare, hoping that I'd been imagining things and he couldn't see through my disguise. The living spirit mages stood out far more than any of the liches did, and there was nothing at all to set me apart from the rest.

His gaze swept around the liches as though taking us all in, before turning back to the front again. Then he raised his voice. "It's an honour to welcome the newcomers to our collective. I'm pleased we've recruited a number of other liches in the last week to replace those we lost, and I hope they remain steadfast in their loyalties."

Oh, crap. It figured he was on full alert, given the fate of the Death King's last spy.

"We allow everyone the chance to join us, regardless of their background," he added. "However, for those of you who came directly from Greyson's collective, I'm going to ask you for a very specific favour."

That's me. And Harper. It didn't escape my attention

that he hadn't called it the Court of the Dead, which backed up the ex-Spirit Agents' implication that he intended to do away with the Death King's Court. Or replace it with his own.

"And what's that?" asked one of the liches.

"Give me your soul amulets," he said.

Shit. I'd rather trust him with my life than with my soul amulet. No way in hell was I letting him get his paws on it.

"What if we refuse?" said the lich who'd spoken. "What if we don't trust you to keep them safe?"

I sent a silent thanks to him for taking the heat off me, because I'd been on the brink of asking the exact same question. Unless I did a Death King and used a fake soul amulet—except his *hadn't* been fake. Twice, he'd used his actual soul as bait. Both times had nearly ended in his death.

I suppressed a groan. *He couldn't have asked us to do anything else, could he?*

"If you don't trust me," he said to the lich, "then you won't get very far. I will give you until tomorrow to think over your decision, along with anyone else who has a problem with my request. All of the new liches, go to that side of the room."

Oh, hell. I wouldn't get very far by faking it this time, so I retreated to the back wall along with the other newbies. At least I stood a better chance at finding Harper this way, but Hawker moved among the crowd like a bird of prey, singling out liches one by one to talk to.

When he approached me, tension gripped me. I'd never been gladder my face couldn't give me away.

"Name?" he said.

"Viva," I replied smoothly.

"You're new here," he said.

"Not the only one." I spoke in a low monotone, but from his lack of reaction, he hadn't recognised my voice. Unless he grabbed my life essence and found me out as a spirit mage, he wasn't to know my true identity.

"You're among the liches who still live in the Death King's castle, correct?" he said.

"If you have another home for outcast dead people somewhere nearby, I'm all ears." I kept my gaze on his face. "Not too many options out there."

"No," he said, "there aren't. I'm sure you understand why I need to take these precautions."

"You aren't afraid the Death King won't have anticipated his liches trying to gain entry into his hall of souls?" I said. "He recently dealt with multiple thefts, and he doesn't let anyone enter aside from a select few. Also, I think he might have a few questions if a whole bunch of us ask for our soul amulets at once."

"You raise a good point," he said. "As it happens, you are in a unique position. You and your fellow liches who risked your lives by coming to me tonight are among the few who have the capacity to offer me insight on the Death King's movements."

"You want me to spy on the Death King for you?" He had to be kidding. The universe had one hell of a sense of irony, that was for sure.

"Yes," he said. "Those of you who still live in the Death King's castle will bring news to me of his movements. If you do, I will allow you to keep your soul amulets in his castle. If not, then you will no longer be welcome here."

"All right," I said. "I don't see the man himself often, but I can certainly give you an insight into his strategies."

I'd bluff if I had to, or perhaps I'd ask the Death King to give me some bullshit cover stories. Anything other than give my soul amulet to the man who'd killed me.

"You're keen," he observed.

"I'm dead," I said. "There's nothing I wouldn't do to return to life. I imagine you understand."

"And you'll find you aren't alone in that," he said. "I understand your pain, Viva. I pretended to serve the Death King for years, and it nearly destroyed my very being."

His words struck me, deep in whatever part of me still had feelings left. *Oh, no.* I was *not* going to sympathise with him. He'd been cursed as a deserved punishment for starting a war, unlike the Death King, who'd been caught up in the backlash through no fault of his own. Not only had Hawker chosen his own fate, here he was, trying to start another war again. Left to his own devices, he'd slaughter us all for his own gain. I had absolutely nothing in common with him whatsoever.

"However," he said, "there's someone else I know the Death King can reach. More than one someone, in fact."

"Oh?" I said warily.

"The Order of the Elements," he said. "On Earth. He is the only lich with permission to access their premises and speak to their members."

Damn. Should have known there'd be a catch. "I thought the Order was under new management."

His eyes narrowed a little at my implication. "There are always growing pains, and it's not always possible for me to visit all my associates in person. We require some of their resources. Can I trust you to get them for me?"

"Depends what they are," I said. "Not like I can lift heavy boxes like this."

He didn't laugh, not that I expected him to. "What we require is information. You may have heard a certain name within the Order... Dirk Alban."

A fresh wave of chills crashed over me, bringing a taste of genuine dread. *Does he know who I am?*

"Wasn't he killed ten years ago?" I was impressed at my voice for staying steady. "I thought it was public knowledge."

"Yes," said Hawker. "He and his fellow spirit mages nearly succeeded in taking over the Order and bringing about our revival. However, when he died, the Order erased him from existence. Some say they killed him themselves. Others say one of his allies turned on him. Whatever the case, we are in need of the Order's official reports on this individual."

We? Was he using it in the royal sense, or did he have another ally, an equal, who I wasn't aware of?

"Don't you already have informants?" I knew I was pushing my luck by bringing it up, but he seemed to make no secret of his network of spies everywhere. "I was under the impression you did."

"The dead can get into places the living cannot," he said. "I intend to send in a group of liches to the Order to gain the knowledge we need. You won't be alone. I'll hand-pick several others, too."

"I'm curious as to why you chose me," I said. "Since I'm new here."

"You're bold," he said. "The others are followers, keen

to let me lead their way. You? You *want.* I know that hunger. I feel it."

"That so?" He couldn't know I hungered to destroy him, as much as I hungered to return to life. My mind remained my own, even if he'd taken away my body, my *life.*

"I think I do," he said. "Come here tomorrow night. Do not say a word of this to the Death King."

He turned away to speak to another lich. I hovered on the spot, unable to shake the creeping feeling of dread. I'd been so certain he'd see through me, and in a way, he had. He'd sensed my longing to be alive again, and if I wasn't careful, he'd use it against me without ever knowing my true identity.

I needed to find Harper and get the hell out of here. The room had begun to empty, so I approached the spot where I'd left Harper the first time around and scanned the shadowy figures hovering around the room.

"Hey," Harper's voice came from nearby. "Is that you, Viva?"

"There you are." I picked out the right lich and approached her. "We really need name tags."

"Yes, we do," she said. "What did Hawker want?"

"He didn't talk to you, then?"

"Nope," she said. "I'm glad, I think. C'mon. We can talk later."

The pair of us drifted over to the transporter, and I could feel the pulse of energy from the machine before the light carried us away to the relatively empty room of Arcadia's citadel.

In silence, we left the room and descended the spiralling staircase to the exit. The walls downstairs were covered in runes, too, though lacking the smooth machinery of the upper floor. Strange how so many of the spirit mages' creations had endured. Hawker might have helped build this place himself, for all I knew.

When we passed out of the exit and into the night, some of the tension leaked out of me like releasing a held breath. Harper floated alongside me across the square, and we'd almost reached the node when two human figures left the citadel behind us. The two spirit mages I'd spoken to earlier. Neither of whom, they'd said, lived in Arcadia.

I leaned closer to Harper. "I think we're being followed."

The two spirit mages were slower than we were, but they also possessed the ability to manipulate the nodes and over my decomposing corpse was I leading them back to the Death King's territory. I floated past the node instead, as did Harper, heading for the pub called the Withered Oak which lay down another side street. As we turned a corner, I glanced behind me again. The pair of them were definitely following us. That, or walking to the tunnels running beneath the city, but I doubted so.

As they neared the corner, I turned to face the two strangers.

"Hey, there," I said. "Thought you weren't local to Arcadia."

"No," he said. "I just recognised your voice."

Shit. He was looking at Harper, not me.

"You got it wrong." Harper looked at him directly, but the faintest tremor underlaid her words. "I don't know you."

"I think you do." His hands sparked with white energy.

"I heard about a rat from the House of Fire who killed Davies and got Flare arrested."

Crap. These mages knew Brant... and Davies, the Death King's ex-Fire Element.

The spirit mage's attack soared past Harper as she dodged with swift lich speed, while the second guy came at me. At once, I thrust a hand into his chest, and grabbed onto his life force. He struggled like a fish in a net, and the tugging sensation would have taken me off my feet if I'd had them. As it was, I tightened my grip, my energy reserves far deeper than they'd been previously.

"See how you like being dead," I snarled.

Light flooded me, and I reeled back, overwhelmed by the current of energy. I folded in on myself in an effort to keep it under control. The mage's body dropped to the ground, his eyes empty and sightless.

His taller buddy paled and tried to run, but I caught up to him with ease and grabbed the threads of his life essence in my hands.

"Shit," he said. "You were a spirit mage, right? I didn't know. Look, forget this ever happened—"

"I *am* a spirit mage," I told him. "You, on the other hand, won't be returning from death."

His struggling grew weaker, while his life force flooded me, as invigorating as stepping into a node. Humming with energy, I let his body fall to the ground.

Harper wheeled to face me. "Damn. He was stronger than I expected."

"He was a spirit mage." I looked at his sightless eyes, his empty expression, and felt... nothing. "I had to kill them both. They would have exposed us to Hawker."

"I know, but what are we supposed to do with the bodies?"

I scanned the narrow street. "Throw them down into the tunnels over there."

We did so—with difficulty, given our incorporeal state. Neither of us could pick the two men up, so I settled for using the node's energy to push the bodies along inch by inch until they tumbled down the tunnel's entrance into the darkness.

"We should go," I said. "If anyone finds them... well, the Spirit Agents already know they're traitors. If anything, Miles will thank us for dealing with them first."

She didn't reply, but it was hard to know if she was at all disturbed by what I'd done. Being a lich was easier than I'd ever imagined, and I wouldn't lie, it was refreshing to be able to use spirit magic openly, without the slightest hesitation.

Yet a part of me couldn't help but wonder... would I ever be able to go back to being human after this?

I led the way back to the node, and we returned to the swampland in silence. The dark shape of the castle loomed overhead as the pair of us drifted through the gates. Harper didn't stop, but floated away into the darkness, leaving me alone.

I headed through the front doors and into the entrance hall, unsurprised to find the Death King waiting for me on the dais at the back. In the darkness, I could barely make out his outline, yet one perk of my newfound lich state was the ability to pick up on the location of other liches. I sensed him like the current of a node, a cold presence which felt more alive than a dead man had the right to.

"What happened?" he said, correctly guessing the night had not gone as planned.

"I killed two spirit mages who recognised Harper on the way back from the citadel," I replied. "They used to be with the Spirit Agents, and they knew Harper from the House of Fire. It freaked her out, but she made it back to the castle and disappeared somewhere."

"Not surprising," he said. "Bria will take care of her."

"Bria knows she's dead?"

"Of course she does," said the Death King.

"I ran into someone from the Spirit Agents, too," I added. "Miles. He said he was there to spy on Hawker, not to join him."

"Likely true," said the Death King. "Miles leads Elysium's Spirit Agents and has been dealing with a similar issue with defecting members. I suppose he decided to check it out in person."

"I don't get it," I said. "I mean, I kinda do, but the liches at least have a reason to join Hawker and his allies. The spirit mages already have their freedom. Do they really want to start another war that badly? Don't they remember the last one?"

"Many don't," he responded. "A whole generation was wiped out, and new spirit mages have only known the Parallel in its current fractured state. They've also never been allowed to travel to Earth, so they have good reason to side with the one person who openly opposes the Order."

"Doesn't mean they have to turn on the guy who stuck his neck out for them," I said.

He didn't respond for a moment, though it was beyond me to tell what he was thinking. Maybe he was remembering all those times I'd implied it *was* his fault that he'd ended up in his position. Before I'd found out the truth.

"And how did it go with Hawker?" he asked.

"He spoke to me," I said. "I thought he recognised me, but apparently not. He wanted all of the liches who still live in the castle to bring our soul amulets to him. When I objected on the grounds that you'd get suspicious about all of us wanting to access the hall of souls at once, he gave me another mission instead."

"What mission?"

"I need to get to the Order," I said. "Turns out Hawker wants us to obtain information from them that his allies can't already get."

"The *Order?*" He sounded genuinely surprised. "I realise he and Cobb were never friends, but if he wants information, there's nothing to stop him from asking Holland or one of his allies instead. Are you sure it wasn't a ruse?"

"I think if he'd recognised me, he'd have killed me on the spot," I said. "I already saw the inside of two of his hideouts."

"Two of them?" he said.

"The citadels are portals," I explained. "He has some kind of machinery in there which functions the same as a node, linking them up. We went through this transporter and wound up in Elysium."

"I thought so," he said. "I should have guessed he and his allies had found a way to travel around the Parallel. That's why the attacks are so widespread."

Of course he knew. "Did you say attacks?"

"On mages," he said. "Presumably, those who didn't want to join his cause."

"Now I've thrown two more dead bodies into the mix." I grimaced. "Why not mention the citadels used to be commonly used as portals?"

"They've been out of use for decades," he said.

"Since the war," I guessed. "Then how did he get them working again?"

"You're spying on him for a reason," said the Death King. "Did he tell you anything else?"

"Only that I need to return to the same place tomorrow to meet with the others who are going to the Order," I said. "Assuming he doesn't find out we killed two of his allies, that is. But he didn't pick Harper. He said he was selecting a special team, including me, and… and the information he needs from the Order concerns Dirk Alban."

He was silent for a moment. "You're sure it isn't a trap?"

"No," I said. "It's that or hand over my soul amulet, and I'd rather not end up with it in the wrong hands the way you did."

"I wouldn't advise you to do that, either," he said. "Are you sure you want to go back to the Order, though?"

"Even if we get caught, there's no way they'll recognise me," I said. "I'm dead to them in a literal sense."

The Order didn't know I existed—and they didn't know I was still a threat.

8

I paced around the quadrangle at the academy, my heartbeat thundering in my ears. My nails were bitten to the quick, and dread chased my every step. A shadow fell over my back and I spun around, tensing, but it was only Greyson.

"You okay?" he said. "Why'd you want to meet out here, Liv? What's with the secrecy?"

I squeezed my eyes shut. "I'm sorry, Greyson. There's something… something I haven't told you."

Concern flickered in his eyes. "What is it?"

"I need a spirit mage's help," I said. "Please. It's urgent."

His shoulders stiffened. "You need what?"

"I know—I know you're a spirit mage." I tripped over the words, urgency constricting my throat. "I won't tell a soul, I promise, but I need your help. Someone—a spirit mage—is planning on doing something terrible."

His eyes widened. "What?"

"I can't say any more than that," I mumbled. "You have to trust me."

I didn't hear his reply. Instead, the corridor faded to nothing, and I came back to awareness to find myself hovering in the corner of the break room at the castle. Darkness blanketed the room, and the only sign of my own wakefulness was the absence of the panic which had pursued me through the memory.

It happened again. I'd seen into the past—before my memory loss this time—yet I hadn't learned anything new. *Trust me,* I'd told Greyson, yet now, he wouldn't even tell me what I'd trusted him with. Aside from helping with Dirk Alban's death, of course.

"I'm gonna need more to work with than that," I muttered to the empty room.

The meditative state didn't return, so I drifted out into the deserted corridor. None of the Elemental Soldiers had stirred yet, so I went outside to watch the sun rising over the castle. Then I spotted a tall, pale someone watching the castle through the gap in the gates.

I glided between the two liches on guard duty and halted before the vampire. His smooth features indicated Asian heritage and made him look far younger than his real age, while his carefully combed hair and impeccable suit were undisturbed by the murky swampland, suggesting he'd used the node to travel here.

"Lord Blackbourne," I said. "To what do I owe the pleasure?"

"You're looking well," he said. "For someone in your condition."

Ha ha. "Speak for yourself. Are you here to see the Death King?"

"I assume Greyson is busy," he remarked. "He does have rather a lot of demands on his attention."

"Actually, I still have no idea how he spends his time." I searched his face for hints of his real purpose here. "Is it me you wanted to see? Curious about how I'm dealing with being a lich?"

"You're keeping yourself busy, what with your attempts to spy on Hawker," said the vampire. "I assume that's what you were doing at the citadel, anyway."

Oh, damn. "You were watching me."

The vampire's smile revealed smooth pointed canines. "You're better at spirit magic than you were when you were alive."

If he thought he could ply me with compliments, he was mistaken. "Tell me what you want."

"We made a bargain, in case you've forgotten," he said.

"I haven't remembered any more of my past," I lied—my conversations with Greyson were none of his business. "Nothing concerning what Dirk Alban told me before his death, anyway."

On the other hand, today's trip to the Order might well turn up that information. Assuming it didn't turn out to be a trap, of course.

"How inconvenient."

"You told me my memories were more likely to return when I was close to death, so I suppose I'll have to wait it out," I added. "Unless you've got any more videos lying around?"

"I only have the footage of your trial," he said. "Nothing else. Are you sure you haven't recalled any more details?"

Nothing that's actually useful. He hadn't earned the right to hear about the vision which had come to me the previous night, and besides, my brief chat with Greyson had brought up more new questions than it had answered. "Maybe that's what Hawker wants me to find out when I go to the Order tonight."

The vampire cocked a brow. "He wants you to spy on the Order?"

I'd debate the wisdom of telling him about my mission, but if it spurred the vampires to actually help out for once, maybe it was worth giving him an insight into the risks he was sitting out on by hiding in his safe house while the rest of us ran dangers. "Yeah, he's sending a bunch of us into the Order to dig up old intel on the last attempt to bring back the spirit mages. So if *they* have any more videos, care to tell me where to find them?"

"They don't," said Lord Blackbourne. "The Order's guards never knew I took the video of your trial either, though I imagine some of them will have noticed its absence."

"You'd have thought they'd have come to ask for it back, if they guessed you were the one who took it."

He flashed me a fanged smile. "The footage of your trial is not as valuable as you might believe. All the people who witnessed the events are very much alive."

"And most of them have their memories intact." I hid a grimace. "Yet *you* seem to think the information in the video is valuable enough for you to steal from them."

"How astute." Another flicker of fangs. "My values are not the same as the Order's, in either its past iteration or its present one. I have to admit, I'm curious about what Hawker wants you to look for."

"I won't find out the details until tonight," I told him. "But since Dirk Alban's name came up, there's a chance it might knock a few memories loose."

"Then you'll keep up your part of the bargain, won't you?" he said. "And tell me what you learn."

"I'll tell you what I remember," I said, "but if I learn anything else from the Order themselves, I'm not obligated to confide in you."

I might not be winning any contests for charisma, but if I didn't make things clear, I'd be open for more manipulation from the vampire lord. He might temporarily be my ally, but he'd sell me out in a heartbeat if it'd keep his fellow vampires safe. He had no more reason to trust me than I had to trust him.

His face betrayed no surprise at me for challenging him. "What is it you want?"

"For one thing, you must know the enemy is travelling between the citadels using the transporters," I said. "Why not try to stop them? Their meeting point in Arcadia is right next to your base."

"I'm aware of that," he said. "Greyson agreed with me that it would be far too much effort to drive them out, considering none of us can enter the citadels without being accosted by their entire army."

"What's he playing at this time?" Perhaps it was a mistake to display my annoyance at the Death King in front of the vampire lord, but he must know Lord Blackbourne was intentionally trying to avoid taking any responsibility. "I realise the citadel can be barred against outside access, but if you *know* there's a bunch of traitorous liches and spirit mages meeting inside, then there must be something you can do."

"Vampires are not permitted into the meetings, and therefore cannot enter the citadels," he said. "Liches are, however, as are spirit mages, so I trust Greyson to share any pertinent information with me. As for myself, I have other strategies in play."

"Like…?"

"Is that what you wish to know?" he said. "My strategies? I'd prefer not to hand out that information for free."

Even as a lich, the vampire lord's tendency to turn everything into a game gave me a headache. "Actually, what I'd like to know is how Hawker circumvented the downsides of the Crow's cantrips in order to bring himself back to life without falling to pieces."

"I told you," he said, "the Crow kept his secrets hidden from the rest of us. We didn't even know he used to be a spirit mage before the war."

"Other vampires were allied with the Crow, though," I pointed out. "Brant went to a high-society event held by vampires where the Crow tricked him into signing over his soul. The Crow can't have been the only vamp in attendance. More of your people were involved, right?"

A smirk tilted his mouth. "You are certainly bolder as a lich than you were as a human, but identifying traitors among my ranks is harder than it may seem. We do value our privacy."

That figured.

"You must be concerned about those cantrips with the potential to kill the dead making a resurgence, surely," I pressed. "And what about the ones Cobb stole from the Order? He even had cantrips with the power to switch off nodes."

"If you're concerned about the Crow's cantrips," he said, "there is someone else who might offer you some insight."

"And who might that be?"

"Your fire mage friend, of course," he said.

Huh? "Brant? You mean I can talk to him?"

"I assumed you'd forgotten him," he said. "Sad, considering he thought you were permanently dead, though perhaps he deserved to suffer for a while."

"Excuse me?" I said. "I don't appreciate you making assumptions about either of us. Might have escaped your attention that I've had enough to deal with. Besides, if he thought I was permanently dead, you could easily have told him otherwise."

"Perhaps you haven't changed as much as I thought," he said, in thoughtful tones. "Even in death, you care for the fire mage."

"Who I care for is none of your business." Why in the Elements' names had I made a deal with this guy? Oh, right, because my life and my friends' safety had been in dire straits at the time.

"Your sense of righteous indignation remains intact, I see," he said. "If you aren't careful, others will see through your disguise."

To be honest, it was something of a relief to know being a lich hadn't entirely stamped out my personality. I could thank the vampire for that, if nothing else. On the other hand...

"You can't still tell I'm a spirit mage, can you?" If he could, then Hawker would be able to do the same, but if that was the case, you'd think he'd have acted against me right away. Not invited me to a top-secret mission to the Order.

"You're glowing with spirit energy," he said. "It's quite noticeable. I suspect it might be due to the punishment you inflicted on those two spirit mages yesterday. Did they guess what you were?"

I thought back. "Only after I killed the first one."

Then Hawker hadn't known. Small mercies. If I was still glowing, though, I'd have to ask the Death King how to get rid of it. It'd be some use getting all the way to an important mission only to expose my real identity at the worst possible moment.

As though conjured up by our words, the Death King glided out of the gates behind me. "Lord Blackbourne."

"Ah, there you are, Greyson," he said. "I was just talking to Olivia here."

"So I see." His gaze travelled over the pair of us. "Anything I need to know?"

"He was going to let me talk to Brant," I said. "About the enemy's plans, particularly with regard to the cantrips. Might be worth hearing what he has to say before I go to the Order tonight."

"I see." The slightest hint of irritation underlaid his voice. "Are you sure the fire mage has useful information?"

"He might," I said. "I'd also like to know how much help I can expect from the vampires if everything goes to shit."

"As much as we can offer, provided you keep your word," said Lord Blackbourne. "Do come with me, Olivia."

I felt the Death King watching my back as I followed him, though I had zero clue what he was thinking. He'd never liked Brant, even before his betrayal. I could examine the many reasons why that might have been, or I could wait for more sensible time. Dealing with my ex-boyfriend would be difficult enough on its own, especially if he'd only recently learned I was still alive.

Lord Blackbourne led the way through the node, and we emerged near the centre of Arcadia. The citadel appeared deserted by day, and though its lack of windows concealed the interior, I never would have guessed that it might contain a portal that linked to the other citadels. The remnants of the spirit mages' old technology I'd seen in there weren't like anything I'd seen on Earth, but Hawker had been alive in the time of the war. He must have figured out how to get the machinery working again since his return from death, and I wouldn't deny that it grated on me that the vampires had done nothing whatsoever to stop him from rebuilding it after the recent battle.

I followed Lord Blackbourne towards the vampires' council house, a squat building with dark curtains covering its windows. The vampire unlocked the polished wooden door and strode ahead down the hallway, while I followed him past the room in which we'd met previously. Elegantly carpeted in red and equipped with smooth mahogany fittings, the place oozed decadence and wealth.

Down a staircase, we emerged in a prison which looked decent enough, by the Parallel's standards. Compared to the Death King's jail, it was practically a palace. A half-dozen cells lined each wall, each wide and spacious. Most were empty, but Brant sat on a bench inside the cell on my right.

He lifted his head when I walked into view. His hair had grown longer, while his stance held a vulnerability that hadn't been there before. Not only had he lost his freedom, he'd also lost his magic. The Order had taken it from him during his last phase in captivity, and with it, they'd stripped away his connection to the magical world. If he left this cell, he was as good as dead.

Despite the instinctual rush of sympathy at the sight of him, I couldn't forget how he'd screwed me over, multiple times. A cacophony of emotions rose within me, much as I tried to deny them.

"What do you want?" he rasped. "Has he sent you to kill me?"

Puzzlement flickered through me, then the truth dawned. He thought I was a lich. I took care to keep my voice as normal as possible when I spoke. "I came here of my own accord."

Brant startled upright. "Liv?"

"Enjoying captivity?" I asked. "I have to admit it's nicer than the Order's cells in here. And much nicer than the Death King's jail, too."

He slumped onto the bench again. "You came here for a reason, didn't you? You haven't visited me yet, not even to tell me you were still alive. Lord Blackbourne had to tell me, and he *laughed* at me when he said you were a lich now."

A smidgeon of pity tempered my annoyance. "Look, I'm *dead.* That takes some adjustment."

"I know." He cleared his throat. "Elements, Liv, I'm so sorry. I thought... I thought you died for real. It took two weeks for me to learn that you survived. Why didn't you *tell* me?" His voice cracked on the last sentence.

"I assumed you knew." Guilt laced my words despite my best efforts. "I thought the vampires would have told you after the battle. I didn't know I was even allowed to visit, and since I came back..."

"You've been serving the Death King," he said. "I

know."

"The Death King's the one who saved me from certain death," I said. "Anyway, I'm here for information."

"On what?" he said. "I have nothing I can offer you. I haven't left this cell since Lord Blackbourne brought me in. I don't know a damn thing that's happening in the city, let alone outside of it."

"I beg to differ," I said. "You were working with Hawker's team, even before you knew who was really in charge."

He flinched. "I told you, I didn't mean to end up drawn into it. He—"

"Don't start with the guilt-tripping," I interrupted. "I've no time for bullshit, Brant. It's not like you've got anything to lose by telling me."

Low blow, maybe, but Brant had dug his own grave... in his case, a metaphorical one.

"I wasn't allowed access to anything important," he said. "It's the truth. The Crow stored his cantrips in my safe house because it was in a convenient location. He didn't confide anything in me."

"You're sure that's all?" I said. "Because it seems like the Crow's cantrips have had a major upgrade recently."

He folded his hands on his lap. "You want to come back to life. I wish I could help, but I don't know how Hawker did it. He was barely involved in my business with the Crow."

"Funny, I didn't get that impression when he damn near murdered me inside your safe house." My voice dropped to a chill, and he cringed away.

"Liv, I swear I didn't know." A pleading note entered his tone. "The Crow was the one who recruited me. I assumed Hawker was just in it for revenge on the Death King."

"He's been around for longer than the Crow has, Brant." Even if he didn't know, there must be something he could tell me which might help. "Since the war, even. How has he been able to bring himself back to life after this long?"

"I wish I knew," he said. "I thought they never got past the downsides of those cantrips. Whatever he used must have come from somewhere else, not the Crow's place."

"What about the other vampires who attended the event you were at when you signed over your soul?" I said. "Are any of them still alive?"

"Probably," he said. "Lord Blackbourne already gave me a grilling. It's not like anyone used their real names. Even the Crow went by a different name when he dealt with the other vampires."

"That figures," I said. "And the cantrips Cobb stole from the Order? Know where they ended up?"

"No," he said. "I haven't heard a word on the Order at all. Are they back open after the attack?"

"As far as I know." Telling him of my espionage mission tonight probably wasn't wise, but it wasn't like he had contact with his allies from here in jail. Besides, maybe I could shock an answer out of him. "Hawker's people can't have complete control, otherwise he wouldn't have to send us to gather intel for him in person."

His brow furrowed. "Send you? You're… no. Liv, you can't be serious."

"Well?" I said. "Any idea what he might be after?"

"He didn't tell you?" He rocked back against the wall.

"Liv, I can't pretend I understand what you're going through, but I was a lich once, too. It's horrible, being like that, but it's better than permanent death. You can't seriously be pretending to support Hawker?"

"My choice, Brant," I said sharply. "It's this or stay as a lich forever. Tell me what you know."

"I don't," he said. "I mean, perhaps there's an area of the Order Cobb and his allies couldn't get at, but I assume Hawker has clearance to go anywhere he likes."

"For whatever reason, he doesn't want to go in person," I said. "Maybe he's too busy plotting world domination."

"Those escaped criminals are still at large, too," he said. "Lord Blackbourne said the Order hasn't given an update on how many of them have been caught."

Crap. I'd forgotten the mass jailbreak, though it explained where some of the spirit mages at Hawker's gathering had come from. Aside from the Spirit Agents, that is. Though there'd been fewer spirit mages who'd once been liches than I'd expected, which did not bode well for my hopes that I'd get to be one of the few to return to life.

Of course, I couldn't discount the possibility that Hawker was testing us, not trying to get genuine intel. That or he wanted us to talk to his allies within the Order, which might cause problems if said allies turned out to be anyone who'd interacted with me when I'd been alive. Though perhaps I was safe, considering Hawker hadn't been able to figure out who I was.

"Not all of them are at large," I said to Brant. "Some of the Crow's allies got recaptured."

"Liv." He leaned forwards. "This isn't how I wanted it

to go, you know that, right?"

His soft tone plucked at something inside me, and I found myself glad of the mask hiding my face. "I'm leaving now."

"Good luck, Liv," he said softly, but I was already turning away from his cell.

As I glided out of the jail, Lord Blackbourne waited at the top of the stairs. "Productive chat?"

"Not really," I said. "Thanks for letting me talk to him, though. I take it he's off the list for execution?"

"Provided he behaves himself," said the vampire. "A fire mage without any magic is hardly a threat to any of us, least of all me."

So he didn't think Brant would team up with the enemy again. Maybe I didn't either, but it surprised me to find how little I cared. I might be glad he hadn't died, but if today had hammered one fact home, it was that whatever feelings I'd had for Brant had departed along with my soul.

———

Upon returning to the castle, I found Ryan in the break room, polishing their sword. Aria and Mav flew out of sight when I walked in, while Dex descended to meet me.

"There you are," the fire sprite said. "Where have you been?"

"To the vampires' jail," I told him. "Lord Blackbourne generously let me ask Brant a couple of questions."

"You visited *fire-boy?*" he said. "You know, I have more firepower than he does now. More's the pity."

"Yeah, he's pretty beaten down," I said. "I wanted to

know what else he knew about Hawker, but he's not exactly up to speed on recent events."

"Good," said Ryan. "The less he knows, the better."

"Well… I did tell him about tonight's mission to the Order," I said. "But that's because I'm struggling to make heads or tails of why Hawker's sending me there."

"The *Order?*" squeaked Dex. "Hawker wants you to go *there?* Are you gonna haunt your old co-workers?"

"Not if I can avoid it," I said pointedly. "I wouldn't have agreed to it, but it was that or let Hawker babysit my soul amulet."

Ryan sheathed their sword at their waist. "But you're still going alone."

"I can come with you," offered Dex. "I've been wondering how the Order's getting along with their new management."

"Hawker would definitely figure out my identity if he saw you hanging out with me," I said. "Not many liches have a fire sprite for a sidekick."

"Would he?" said Dex. "Has he ever met me?"

"He's certainly seen us together," I said. "So has Cobb, come to that."

"I doubt Cobb will be there," Ryan said. "I know the Order pardoned him, but if he has any sense, he'll be staying away in case someone realises the prison breakout coincided with the attack on your school reunion."

"Fair point," I said. "You can't come with me, though. I think the other liches will notice an Air Element following me around. More than a fire sprite, even."

Ryan scowled. "I think this is a trap. Why would Hawker need you to go to the Order? His allies are in control of the place."

"I told you, it's about Dirk Alban," I said. "Hawker didn't witness his death. He also didn't get the chance to talk to him beforehand, I assume, if he was hiding here in the Court of the Dead while Alban and his allies tried to take over the Order."

"So he thinks the Order hid information in their files," they said in sceptical tones.

I shrugged. "They don't know Lord Blackbourne stole the video of my trial."

"Did he mention *why* he took it?" Ryan said.

"Nope," I said. "He also said I'm glowing because of the energy I took from those spirit mages, so I need to figure out how to get rid of that before tonight."

"Yeah, you are glowing a bit," said Dex. "You can come and shoot down some phantoms with me."

"Might have to take you up on that offer," I said. "Where's Harper, do you know?"

"She decided to sit this one out," said Ryan. "Gave up being a spy, according to Bria. Can't say I blame her."

"Me neither," I said. "It'd have been nice to have backup at the Order, but maybe it's better if I go alone. In case it turns out to be a trap."

"I can be your lookout," Dex said. "Come on. Let me have my fun."

"If you're careful, then I might let you come." It might be useful to have him there, especially if Hawker's allies turned on me. The Order was not a good place to be as a lich generally, and if I ran out of strength away from the nodes, I might find myself in a world of trouble.

Besides, despite what Lord Blackbourne said, I didn't want to do this alone.

9

Once again, I set off for the citadel under cover of night. When I left the castle, the fire sprite flew up to join me. "Ready?"

"Hey, Dex," I said. "Can you ask Mav to keep an eye on Harper? I'm kinda worried about her."

"Oh, she already told me Harper wants to lie low for a bit," he said. "Since you keep attracting trouble."

"Hey, I'm going on this mission alone anyway," I said. "Except for you, of course. We're going to meet the others at Arcadia's citadel, so be quiet, okay?"

"We're going to the citadel." He flew around in excited circles while I crossed the swamp, only calming down when we emerged from the node in the centre of Arcadia.

We approached the citadel, while I shushed him. "Please keep out of sight or else we're both screwed."

"What do you take me for?" he whispered in my ear. "I'll behave."

"Just remember it'll be a lot harder for you to hide behind me now I'm like this," I reminded him.

"I can still hide inside your cloak."

Warmth singed my shoulder. "Please don't. You know liches aren't inflammable, right? I don't need to combust before we even start the mission."

The door swung open and both of us clammed up as the usual lich greeted me. "Viva. Your friend isn't here?"

"She decided to sit this one out," I said, hoping he couldn't see Dex glowing under my cloak. "I'm here to meet with Hawker's team to go to the Order."

"Good," he said. "The rest of the team's already here."

He gestured to the room within, where several liches gathered, all identical. I drifted over to join them, trying to pick out features to tell them apart by, but even their voices sounded similar. At least I wouldn't stand out in any way.

"What does Hawker want us to find at the Order?" I asked the liches. "Something that requires us to walk through walls?"

"Don't look at me," said one of the others. "The Order specifically requested liches, he said."

"Wonder why he picked us?" Nothing leapt out at me about the other liches' appearances, though I also wouldn't have been able to tell if any of them were spirit mages, which was reassuring enough for my own cover, at least.

"We're all here," said the leading lich. "Let's move."

We left the tower, drifting across the square towards the node once again. In a swarm of shadow, we passed through it, emerging into the darkness of Birmingham city centre.

The Order's headquarters came into view, and a weird sense of nostalgia washed over me at the sight of the ordinary office blocks, and the place which had held me in its grip for my entire adult life. The entire world held a sense of unreality, as though I watched from the other side of a glass pane, the sounds and sights both subdued and yet clearer than they'd ever been in life. While the node thrummed beneath me, I knew it wouldn't last once we moved away. *Better hope my lich form is tough enough to survive this.*

"I'll go ahead and scout for trouble," Dex said in my ear.

While Dex flew out of sight, I joined the others in approaching the Order's headquarters. Away from the node, I didn't feel noticeably weaker, though I'd have a hell of a time defending myself if all the other liches turned on me at once. At least I didn't feel on the verge of falling to pieces without the node's presence nearby, though a sense of vulnerability tugged at me the further we travelled from the current of energy.

The security guards outside the Order's headquarters didn't challenge us, though they gave us uneasy looks and kept their distance as our group swept through the doors in a mass of darkness. Inside the building, the lobby looked the same as usual. I didn't know if I'd expected to see Cobb sitting on a throne or something, but it was as though nothing had changed at all. Maybe it was a little quiet, but that was to be expected in the evening when only the delivery crew and people returning from missions were here. I marvelled at how everyone carried on as if nothing had happened, willingly or unwillingly aiding the enemy. Even if there were more of the latter than the former, I wondered how much overlap there was with the people who'd jumped at the chance to punish me for illegally learning spirit magic.

Did any of them know the spirit mages were now running the show?

It came as a surprise when the leading lich led us to the office which had once belonged to Mr Cobb, and none other than Mr Holland waited on the other side. The head interrogator had neatly trimmed grey hair and sideburns, while his spectacles highlighted his clear grey eyes. He matched me in height even as a lich, and for an instant, I was certain he saw the person beneath my mask. Then my fear evaporated as if it'd never existed. He couldn't force me to sit through an interrogation as he had once before. He couldn't threaten me with death or imprisonment. He was nothing more than a human, without an ounce of magic to his name.

"Everyone here?" said Mr Holland. "Good. Come with me."

Tension gripped me when he led the way to the elevator. I did *not* want to follow the bastard into an enclosed space, yet I'd promised to see this through. *He can't hurt you. None of them can.*

The tide of liches carried me into the lift, and we travelled down until we reached the lower floor. The door slid open, revealing a corridor I recognised from when I'd come here looking for answers once before. While the oppressive sensation in the air wasn't quite as potent as a lich as it had been when I'd been human, a pressure stifled me on every side. I held my breath, ready for scenes from my past to start replaying, but nothing happened this time. Just the same persistent cold sensation pressing against my non-existent body, along with the emptiness of not being able to access the node.

That was the difference. My spirit magic was almost entirely cut off down here, with no nodes within reach. I took back my earlier thoughts about the Order not being able to do us harm and wished I'd sacked the whole thing off and spent the evening watching the Elemental Soldiers play video games instead.

No. I have to do this.

We rounded a corner, tailing Holland past a row of cells to another corridor panelled in dull metal with doors on either side. I'd been tried as a spirit mage in one of these rooms. More recently, Cobb had trapped me here and tried to force another spirit mage to rip out my soul.

Yet all those thoughts fled when I saw who guarded the door at the corridor's end: none other than Judith French. She couldn't know who I was, surely, but I struggled to rein in my curiosity about how in the world she'd wound up working down here. She was only a practitioner, yet she wore the grey uniform of a prison guard and stood stiffly outside a partially see-through door I'd never been through before. On the other side, gleaming metal walls and fluorescent lights painted a chillingly familiar picture.

Mr Holland led us around another corner until he came to a halt outside a room panelled in metal and gleaming with light. Another uniformed guard stood outside, and Holland stepped in to speak to him.

"These liches have generously volunteered to help you," said Holland.

"Have they?" said the guard in a disinterested voice.

"We've almost perfected the spell. There's no need for any more volunteers."

What the hell is this? I glanced behind me, but more guards had moved to block our way back down the corridor. I surreptitiously reached for the nearest wall to see if I could float through it and found a solid surface beneath my hand.

Oh, hell. The magic-proofed walls also apparently kept out liches, too.

"This way." Holland beckoned to the lich at the front of the group. "One at a time. This shouldn't take long."

I peered through the glass door and spotted two other Order employees inside the room, each holding a gleaming cantrip in their hand. If the other liches suspected the ruse, nobody said a word. The first lich left the group and the door opened to let them in.

Energy sparked between the two cantrips as the lich entered the room. A light flared, and the lich exploded into dust. Holland clapped his hands, while the other liches recoiled, an air of stunned disbelief rippling through our group.

"There," he said, in a carrying whisper. "No need to involve any soul amulets, either."

No soul amulets?

This must be how they'd killed the spies from the Court of the Dead. He was using the Order as his secret lab to test out cantrips to use against the liches, and as we'd dared to question Hawker, he'd volunteered us as lab rats.

As Mr Holland ushered another lich into the room, I shifted backwards through the group. Mutters broke out among them, and as the second lich exploded into a pile of dust, their panic grew. Behind us, the guards moved closer, cantrips gleaming in their own hands, while the magic-proofed walls held us captive.

"I wouldn't," said Mr Holland. "There's no way out from here. You had your chance to prove your loyalty, and you failed."

Dammit. I shuffled backwards through the group, and then, to my intense relief, I spotted a spark of light at the corridor's end. Dex had come downstairs to check up on me. Pity I couldn't signal to him without drawing attention.

Thankfully, years of running missions together had given him a good instinct for timing, and when Holland turned to talk to the guard again, Dex raised his hands and shot a fireball into the air.

Sparks of light ricocheted off the ceiling, and the guards exclaimed, backing down the corridor in search of their attacker. *Thanks, Dex.*

I turned heel and got the hell out of there with all the speed I possessed. Dex flew up to me as I glided around a corner, and I breathed a thanks in his general direction.

"Help the others," I whispered, without slowing down. "They didn't volunteer to die any more than I did."

I turned the corner as I spoke, and Judith's head swung in my direction. *"Liv?"*

Oh, bugger. Nothing for it. I thrust my hand into her chest and grabbed her life force.

Judith gasped. "Help—"

"Scream and I'll drain you in a second," I hissed.

"It *is* you," she breathed. "Liv. You're… one of them."

I didn't let go. "And you're working with Cobb."

"What?" she said. "Cobb is in jail."

"Haven't you noticed he's no longer in his cell?" I said in a low voice. "He escaped. Got the upper room to pardon him and now his buddy Holland is running the show."

She shook her head. "You're lying."

"I'm not," I said. "You know those liches you just saw? Holland brought them here to kill them for disobeying Hawker. They're all conspirators. And if you're willingly helping them out, you're complicit as well."

At that moment, several other liches glided into view, pursued by the guards. I swore and dropped Judith, who pointed mutely ahead. I ran down the corridor and spotted an 'emergency exit' sign ahead. Silently thanking whatever part of her conscience had won out, I picked up speed, and the other liches joined the tide fleeing for the exit.

Then we halted, finding our path barred by two cantrip-wielding Order employees. I spun around, but two more guards blocked our way back. If we'd been near a node, I might be able to take them on, but the place felt utterly devoid of any spirit energy whatsoever. Yet the cantrips in the guards' hands were in full working order, and if they used them on me, my life would come to an end. This time, for good.

A spark appeared in the corner of my eye and heat singed my shoulder as Dex flew over to join us. "What do you want me to do? I can't stop them all at once."

Oh, boy. One way out remained, but damn, this was going to hurt.

"Dex," I breathed. "When I say now, set the corridor on fire."

"You're in the way," he hissed back.

"I don't care," I told him. "This is the only way out. Start a fire, then fly like hell."

I heard him cursing in my ear. Then a torrent of flames leapt in front of me, catching the nearby liches in their grasp. The guards broke formation as the fire spread among us. Flames engulfed me from head to toe, and the world turned to ashes and pain.

10

Dying a second time was even more uncomfortable than the first. Flames licked at my non-existent skin, and I had a brief moment of disorientation where I found myself hovering in the air without anything to ground me before all went blank.

Then I found myself facing Dirk Alban.

In my other visions of him, I'd only seen fragments, distorted by my hazy memory. This time, all was clear, and it startled me how young he looked, in his early thirties at most. His glossy dark hair, smooth unblemished skin, and polished attire spoke of a lifetime of privilege, yet his soft tone sounded eminently relatable, as though he was confiding a secret for my ears alone.

"Here we are," he said to me. "Ready?"

I nodded. "Sure. I'm ready."

"You're sure you want to learn magic?" he said. "Once you make the choice, there'll be no going back. You also won't be able to tell a single soul about any of this, not even your closest friends."

I licked my lips. "I understand."

"But know this," he went on, "if you stay on your path and join the Order of the Elements, you'll never be allowed to use your powers. Your talent will die on the vine, and your future will remain in their hands."

I said nothing. I knew he was right, after all.

"I know what you want, Olivia," he said. "I can sense it. You have a talent, and you long to express it. The Order will never give you that chance. They can't know. This will be our secret."

The scene broke apart, shattering like glass, replaced with visions of a metallic reflective wall streaked with blood. Dirk Alban's screaming echoed in my ears. *"You ruined everything, Olivia. You ruined it..."*

When I came back to full awareness, I found myself floating inside the hall of souls. I glanced down, seeing the usual shadowy cloaked form where my body had once been. I looked exactly the same as I had before I'd been set ablaze. It appeared that my regenerative powers were in full working order. Endless rows of golden discs filled the shelves on either side of me, emanating a faint glow.

I rotated on the spot and saw the Death King watching me, tall and silent. I damn near jumped out of my skin— or I would have done if I'd had skin to jump out of. "How long have you been here?"

"Not long," he said. "What did you do, Olivia?"

"I asked Dex to set the corridor on fire, burning me and the other liches in the process," I said. "It was the only way for me to get out of there in one piece without dying permanently. Hawker is turning any liches who question him into lab rats, in order to test the spell which killed your last spies."

"I did wonder," he said, in a deceptively calm tone. "It felt too soon for a major mission. Hawker was smarter than that."

"I guess I challenged him too openly," I said. "I suppose the liches who handed over their soul amulets were allowed to carry on. Those of us who objected paid the price."

"He'll know you survived, but not how to recognise you," he added. "Better to lie low, like Harper."

"Harper's okay, isn't she?"

"She backed out of being a spy for the foreseeable future," he said. "She's helping Bria instead."

"Good," I said. "Um, helping her with what?"

Dex floated into the room. "That was *not* cool, Liv. I thought I'd toasted you."

"Sorry," I said. "If you ask me, we got lucky. It's only a matter of time before they bring those cantrips to the castle. Any lich who refuses to join them will probably meet the same fate."

"I'd like to see them try," said the Death King.

"I'd rather avoid it, thanks." I turned to Dex. "I'm glad you got out."

"Barely," he said. "Those spells they had would have destroyed me along with the rest of you. I'm lucky they didn't see me."

"I wish there'd been another way to escape," I said, "but honestly, getting set on fire is better than being obliterated by a lich-killing spell. So much for him recruiting liches to save them from an early death."

The doors crashed open and Ryan burst into the hall of souls. "Liv?"

I gave a wave. "That's me."

"Thank the Elements," they said. "I heard you died."

"I did," I said. "But I'm still alive. Or as alive as most of us get in this place, anyway."

"Your soul amulet is in one piece?" they said.

"It might not stay that way if you leave the door open," the Death King interjected. "Please refrain from getting killed again."

I rolled my eyes as he left. "Better get out of here. I think my soul is just fine."

"I should bloody hope so." If anything, Ryan looked even more rattled than me. "I never paid attention to how long it takes a lich to regenerate before, but Dex was barely coherent when he came in."

"It was a very traumatic experience," he said.

"I said I was sorry," I said. "Anyway, I guess Hawker and I aren't going to be buddies after all."

"So he went to the trouble of singling you out for a special mission only to have you killed?" said Ryan.

"Looked that way," I said. "Anyway, I think it's a safe bet that Holland and his allies are planning on using their lich-killing cantrips here in the Parallel as well."

"Did anyone recognise you?" asked Ryan.

"Ah, shit," I said, remembering. "Judith French. We were classmates at the academy, and she's wanted a top position at the Order for ages. She's the one who kept showing up at Devon's shop trying to catch us breaking the Order's rules."

They pulled a face. "I know the type."

"She did point me to the exit when I was trying to escape the Order's guards, for some reason," I added. "Granted, she might have told tales on me after I vanished, so I won't speak too soon. Anyway, Dex torched the whole corridor. Pity he didn't hit Holland in the process."

"Who even is this Holland person?" asked Ryan.

"Head interrogator," I said. "Now he's been promoted to the upper room. I don't think he's a spirit mage, though. He's a plain old human who just wants power."

"And to destroy the liches," Dex put in. "Little shit. I should have set his shoes on fire, but I was more concerned with getting away from those cantrips."

"Just be glad we both got out," I said.

"By dying," Ryan said dryly. "You know, I see why the Death King finds you so frustrating."

I followed them through the hall, noticing that someone had stuck googly eyes and fake moustaches on some of the skulls which formed the pillars.

"Who did that?" I asked.

"Our new Fire Element," Ryan said, with an expression of distaste.

The new décor was an improvement, I'd admit, but the Death King's trust of Bria still made as little sense to me as ever. Maybe he was actually planning on using *her* as a lab rat. It was anyone's guess at this point.

In any case, my narrow escape had unnerved me more than I'd expected, even though my soul amulet had remained intact. Hawker hadn't figured out my secret, but he'd tried to have me killed anyway. So much for spying on him.

"Wait, how long has it been?" I asked. "Since I died?"

"Twelve hours, give or take," Ryan said.

"Damn, it must be morning," I said. "I have to speak to Devon. Better advise her not to go to the Order in case Judith did tell everyone there that I was alive."

"I'll come with you," said Ryan. "The Death King hasn't given me any instructions."

"Shouldn't you be guarding the place in case the Order sends people here?" I said.

"Did they mention an upcoming attack on the castle?"

"Well… no," I admitted. "You know Trix probably isn't going to be at Devon's, don't you?"

"I know," they said. "Just felt like playing a social call. I haven't got out of the castle much lately."

After saying goodbye to Dex, the pair of us travelled through the node to the house, where Devon sat playing Skyrim on the Xbox. She hit the pause button when we appeared next to her.

"Hey, Liv," she said. "Oh, and you, too, Ryan. Does nobody knock on the door anymore?"

"You're not going to the Order, are you?" I asked her.

"No," she said. "What happened this time?"

"She died again," Ryan said.

I shot them a glare. "Not the same as last time. The Order cornered me with lich-killing cantrips, and I had to get Dex to incinerate me to get out."

Devon dropped the controller. "You did what?"

I gave her a summary of yesterday's ill-fated mission. When I'd finished, she rolled her eyes. "Fucking Order. I don't even want to take their money at this point, in case they use it to make more of those cantrips."

"Pretty sure they got them from the Crow," I said. "It's how they killed the last spy the Death King sent to join Hawker."

"Damn," she said. "Okay, I can see why you decided you'd be better off being set on fire. I just wish there was a decent way of earning a living as a practitioner without helping the Order."

"Yeah, I know that feeling."

Dirk Alban's words came back to me again. *You want this. You have a talent, and you long to express it. The Order will never give you that chance.*

While I'd joined him willingly, the Order shared some of the blame. Yet if they hadn't banned spirit magic, would Hawker's people have taken power even quicker? Or would he have been deprived of his need for revenge and disappeared from the picture entirely? I didn't know, but there was no use wondering what might have been, had we lived in another time.

Devon yawned. "I wasn't going to check in with the Order anyway, but if they show up here, maybe I should set up a booby trap just in case. Unless Ryan wants to volunteer to chase them off."

"Ryan is supposed to be guarding the castle." I nudged them. "They came here looking for Trix, for some reason."

The Air Element scowled, while Devon blinked at both of us. "Why would he be here at this time?"

"Trix never pays attention to the time of day, but I think there was another motive involved." I gave them another prod.

Ryan stepped aside. "Can you not do that? It feels like you're throwing ice-water all over my arm."

Devon cracked a grin. "You like him. Trix, I mean."

"Of course I like him," said the Air Element. "Not liking Trix is the same as not liking a baby kitten."

"Fair point there," I said, "but you know what she means."

"I know you're annoying."

"Ooh." Devon bounded to her feet. "You want me to break the news to him? Because he'd rather hear it from you, I think."

"How much do you know about elves?" asked Ryan. "Because I'll be honest, I don't have a lot of experience with them. Sometimes I think he gets it, and other times… it's like we're on different wavelengths."

"When do you get on best, then?" she asked.

"When we're talking about our D&D characters," said Ryan. "But that's not… real."

"I don't see why it can't be," Devon said. "If you want me to incorporate a few hints into our game, let me know."

She probably would, too. Devon might be aromantic asexual, but she could dish out relationship advice like nobody's business and had set people up for dates via our gaming sessions before.

"Never mind," Ryan said, going pink. "You should help Liv instead."

Her gaze went to me. "With what?"

"I heard you went back to speak to the fire mage again," Ryan said.

"You spoke to Brant," said Devon. "And?"

"And nothing," I said. "Really nothing."

Ryan blinked at me. "Really… nothing."

"Is that a surprise?" I said. "Whatever we had, it's long gone."

Devon blew out a breath. "Well, I can't say I'm

surprised. You've been to hell and back since he screwed you over."

"I have. Literally." I wanted my life back before I could even begin to think about the future again. "At least I know I can survive incineration."

"Not at Brant's hands, since he has no magic," said Devon. "Weird, that. Magic was his whole identity."

"Yeah, I know." Yet our unexpected shared trauma had only hammered home how much things had changed between us. "We should see if the Death King has any orders for us, Ryan. We don't want him manifesting in here if the Order shows up."

Devon rubbed her eyes. "I'm still working on your illusion cantrips. Let me know if you need any others, okay?"

"Will do."

Ryan and I returned to the swampland via the node and approached the gates, at which point Ryan stopped. Trix stood outside, his bright smile a contrast to the bleakness of the surrounding scenery. "Oh, hello, Ryan. And you, Liv. I heard you were dead. More dead, I mean."

"I know what you mean," I said, resigning myself to half the Parallel knowing by the end of the morning. "I got better."

Ryan approached the elf. "What are you doing out here alone? There are phantoms… wights…"

"I'll be fine," said Trix. "I was trying to make friends with your horse, but he ran away."

I stifled a grin. I'd have nudged Ryan, but they sidestepped and went to give the nearest zombie horse a stroke. I tried to give them a look telling them to go and talk to Trix, but since I still had a severe case of resting lich face, it went unseen.

"Is the Death King not in?" I asked Trix.

"I haven't seen him," he responded, oblivious to Ryan's reluctance to meet his eyes.

"He'd better not be at the Order." Even with his soul amulet still in the castle, those cantrips in the Order's basement were capable of obliterating him. He must know the risks, but the guy was reckless with his own soul amulet at the best of times.

"Maybe she knows," said the elf, looking at the node behind us.

Ryan and I both turned in that direction, where Bria had materialised, clad in her Fire Element gear and carrying a sword which I assumed the Death King had given her.

"Problems?" Ryan queried.

"You might say that." Bria sprinted past us, through the gates to the castle. "Someone attacked the Withered Oak. I'm going to find the Death King."

"The Death King isn't in," Ryan said. "She's not listening, is she?"

"Nope." I peered through the gap in the gates, but Bria had disappeared.

Ryan glanced around the swamp, then strode towards the node.

"You're going to the Withered Oak now?" I called after them. "Whatever happened to asking permission from the boss?"

"Did I ever say I had to?" they said. "I've been cooped up for too long."

I fixed on a grin. "Just admit I'm a terrible influence on you and be done with it."

"Hey, you're the one who gets to go out on espionage

missions," they said. "Want me to fetch that fire sprite of yours to come with us?"

"Dex might still be mad at me after last night," I said. "But I doubt he'll want to miss out."

The two of us walked through the gates, while Trix glided alongside us. He moved kind of like a lich himself, minus the transparency, and Ryan's eyes followed his every movement as we walked. Regardless, they refused to pick up on my pointed looks, so I glided ahead towards the break room. All three sprites were in there, but Dex zeroed in on me as soon as I walked in.

"Do I detect a smidgeon of rebellion in the air?" The fire sprite flew in front of Trix. "What's he doing here?"

"Mages are attacking the Withered Oak," I told him. "Want to come and check it out?"

"Wouldn't miss it." He swooped overhead, calling over his shoulder to Aria, "Can you tell the other Elemental Soldiers where we are?"

"Yes, but please be careful," the air sprite called back.

Trix, Ryan and me retraced our steps out of the castle. The instant our group passed through the node and landed in Arcadia's centre, the smell of burning drifted in our direction.

"That's not good," said Dex. "Was it Bria who raised the alarm, by any chance?"

"Yes… why?" Oh, damn. The pub was on fire *again*, and the faint scent of magic beneath the acrid smoke indicated a magical cause. "Did *she* start the fire?"

"Probably not," he said. "Not if there were innocent people in there. She's been gone all morning, so I figured she'd got herself into trouble."

Ryan approached a group of mages gathering near the

pub, one of whom was the young black guy who assisted the bartender in the Withered Oak.

"What happened here?" asked Ryan.

"Bloody mages," said the bartender's assistant. "Illegal cantrip trade, apparently. I think they just like an excuse to set things on fire."

"Fire mages, by any chance?" I said. "From the House of Fire?"

The man stepped away from me, his expression shifting to fear. "We don't need the Death King involved."

"He isn't." I still hadn't quite got used to the way ordinary people reacted to me, as though they thought I'd rip out their souls, given the chance. They saw me as a spirit mage who'd sold her soul for power. Not someone faced with a terrible situation and no way out. I hadn't done much to mitigate that impression myself, admittedly, but I made a mental note to be nicer to the other liches when I came back to life, no matter how creepy they might look.

"There's someone still inside." Ryan indicated the shadow of a human figure near the Withered Oak's window.

Oh, damn. Only a fire mage would willingly stay in a burning building, so it was safe to say they were not friendly. I moved closer to the door, the heat emanating from within biting through my transparent cloak.

"Two people in there," Dex said in my ear. "Two... and they can see you."

Time to roll initiative. I shoved open the door and faced the mages, who each wielded fireballs in their hands. Good job I no longer needed to breathe, because the heat was uncomfortable enough on its own.

"Liv," Ryan warned. "The place is gonna come crashing down if we're not careful."

"Don't use your magic," I warned. "The fire will spread. I'll take care of them."

"You're with the Death King, are you?" said one of the mages. "Give your master our regards… from hell."

Flames blasted towards us. Ryan held up their hands, conjuring a whirlwind and knocking the fireball straight back at the conjurer. As for me, I sidestepped the whirlwind and closed in on the mage, my hand reaching for his life force. With one quick tug, he was on the ground. Natural twenty, no dice necessary.

I bent over him, casting a long shadow over his fearful face. "Who sent you?"

"Hey there," said Dex to the second mage. "Want some more fire?"

The other mage stumbled into the doorway with a yelp, his clothes catching ablaze. The heat rose, and my transparent cloak started to smoke at the edges. Despite the flames eating away at his own clothing, the mage laughed. "Your master's days are numbered, lich."

I reached out and yanked out the mage's life force, energy flooding me. Invigorated, I spun on the spot and saw the floor in the main area of the bar had split down the middle. Splintered floorboards poked upwards, while a sizeable hole filled the space between. An earth mage had been here, and they'd made their getaway belowground.

I glided over to peer into the hole in the earth. Then a pair of hands reached out and closed around my neck, passing right through my transparent form. I twisted out of reach, grabbing for my attacker's life force.

"You!" shouted the man. "You're one of his. You're the reason we're dead."

"I have no idea what you're talking about." The man was filthy, covered in so much dirt that I couldn't make out his features. "If you don't get out of here, though, you'll end up in an early grave."

"I've already been there," he said. "At the Order."

Recognition hit me like a slap to the face. *Vaughn?* Brant's earth mage friend, who'd been imprisoned for conspiring with the enemy? He must have escaped the Order's jail during Cobb's mass breakout, and it seemed he'd gone straight back to his old habits of illegally trading cantrips.

Dex zipped into the room above my head. "Oh. It's you."

"You!" Vaughn screamed, sounding quite deranged. "You got me locked up."

"You locked *me* in a cage, in case you've forgotten," I yelled back, my voice cold and echoing. "Back to your old tricks again, are you?"

I descended into the hole he'd made in the ground, hand reaching for his life force. Energy flooded me, followed by a searing pain. A grin twisted Vaughn's mouth as fire leapt from a disc-shape in his hand. *He has an inferno cantrip.*

Not again.

The flames drew closer and engulfed me from head to toe, succeeded by a familiar blackness.

11

Dirk Alban's voice spun around me, shouting advice, as I struggled to contain the current of energy blasting out of my hands.

"Come on!" he said. "You can handle it."

"I—can't—" I gasped out.

"Yes, you can," he insisted. "We're built like batteries, we spirit mages are, and the more we draw on, the more power we have. Keep at it, and you'll be able to part oceans and move mountains. You can split the foundations of the earth and rebuild it anew."

My whole being trembled to the core. Pain split my body in half, down to the fabric of my soul.

And then Dirk Alban's soul was in my hands, and blood was on the walls, and he was shouting at me that I'd ruined everything—everything—

I came back to alertness with a gasp. I'd landed in the hall of souls, again, regenerating after my second death in as many days. And… oh, bugger. The Death King stood nearby, radiating menace and disapproval.

"Hey." I straightened upright. "Is Ryan okay?"

"Ryan is fine," he said. "You, on the other hand, seem intent on testing the limit for how many times a lich can regenerate."

"Thought it was infinite," I said. "Unless I'm like a Time Lord."

"I wouldn't push your luck," he said. "What were you thinking?"

"I wanted to know who set the Withered Oak on fire," I said. "I found out where some of the mages Cobb set free were hiding, and they were trading in illegal cantrips, too. Unfortunately, they were a few bricks short of a wall."

"You didn't even consider telling me before running off?" he said, in exasperated tones.

"You were out!" I said. "Bria came to report to you and found us instead. Where even were you?"

"Dealing with some important business," he said. "I should have known better than to leave you unattended in the castle."

"Hey, it was Ryan's idea to go check out the Withered Oak," I protested. "I wasn't gonna let them go alone. Besides, I can go anywhere 'unattended' if I like. I'm not one of your zombie horses."

"You need to remember that you aren't invulnerable," he countered. "Not even as you are now. If you perish, permanently, it'll invalidate everything I did to prevent your death."

"So it's all about you, is that it?" Hot tension simmered in the air despite the chill lingering from my latest encounter with death. "Were you this annoying when we were at school, Grey?"

He stared at me for a moment. "You called me Grey."

"It's your name, isn't it?"

"You've never called me that before."

"Didn't know I had to ask permission." Despite my face being hidden, I had the uncanny sense that he could see more in my expression than I wanted to show. "Who was I to you, Greyson Beaumont? Tell me. Honestly."

"You'll have to find that out for yourself."

Before I could yell at him that it was not cool to run off without answering me, he swept out of sight and left me alone in the hall of souls.

I swore under my breath, then left the room. Dex appeared on the other side of the door, arms folded over his chest. "What are you playing at?"

"What?" I said. "Don't you start on me. I knew liches were flammable, but not *that* much."

"Until you died twice in two days," he said. "I can see why you're driving the Death King into an early grave."

"The Death King has his own issues." To say the least. "What happened to our mage friend, did you see?"

"I think he blew himself up with his own cantrip," he said. "Or got buried alive."

"More's the pity." I drifted through the hall, more unsettled by the Death King's behaviour than by my second death in a twenty-four-hour span. "Okay, maybe I shouldn't have gone into the Withered Oak myself, but if I hadn't, I wouldn't have known Brant's dickhead friend was still around."

"I know you're pretty much fearless now you're all transparent and creepy, but this is starting to become a hobby of yours," said Dex.

"Since when were you the responsible one?" I said to him. "I guess I have to apologise to Ryan again, too."

Outside, night had fallen. As I floated down the stone staircase, I spotted Trix in the grounds, struggling to mount a zombie horse under Ryan's instructions. I stared for a moment at the inexplicable sight.

"Oh, hello, Liv." Trix waved at me. "Welcome back."

Ryan glowered. I tried a smile, but my illusion skills weren't quite back in working order. Instead, I floated down to join them. "Made friends with Neddie, did you, Trix?"

"More like he wanted an excuse to spend time around his favourite Air Element." Dex cackled. "Even though he keeps getting thrown in the mud by a zombie horse."

Ryan scowled, but before they could respond, shouts came from the direction of the gates. Then I spotted Felicity and Cal approaching us, both with their weapons out.

"What's going on this time?" I asked.

Felicity halted in front of me. "Lord Blackbourne is requesting our aid. The vampires are under attack."

"Damn." Looked like the vampire lord's insistence on ignoring the enemy's secret meetings in the citadel had come back to bite him. "Who is it? Hawker's liches? Spirit mages?"

"No idea," Felicity said. "Wouldn't surprise me if it was the same mages who attacked the Withered Oak, though."

I couldn't say Lord Blackbourne hadn't been warned, several times, but if he'd requested our help, he'd be obligated to return the favour later on. While I hadn't met all the vampires in Arcadia, I was pretty sure Hawker's contingent of spirit mages and liches outnumbered them. Not to mention their fighting style was designed to take advantage of the nodes, of which one lay right by the vampires' place. Lord Blackbourne ought to be well aware of that fact and part of me was tempted to leave him to deal with them by himself, but if he died, it'd leave one hell of a power vacuum in the city.

"You aren't coming," Ryan told me. "Mostly because the Death King would murder me if I let you."

"Doesn't the threat of temporary or permanent death get old after a while?" I rolled my eyes. "I'm not sitting this one out. If any fire or spirit mages are involved, I imagine the vampires will come off worse."

I half expected the Death King to appear from the shadows and intervene, but he didn't, not even when I followed the Elemental Soldiers through the gates and towards the node.

The instant we emerged from the current of light near the citadel, energy surged into my hands, aimed at the dark figures approaching the vampires' council hall. Based on the timing of the warning, some of them must already be inside, but their shadowy countenances looked awfully familiar. *Hawker's liches.*

I picked up speed. Magic blasted from my palms and knocked two of the opposing liches sideways. They turned and glided towards me, and I met their challenge gladly. In my previous life, I'd been a better runner than a fighter, but whether human or lich, I was definitely a better fighter than a spy. Especially with my handy new advantages. With one thrust of my palm, I ripped the life force out of the first lich. The second came at me, grabbing for my own life force, but Dex hurled a fireball at him first. He disintegrated into a screaming pillar of flames, and within a few seconds, he turned to ashes and crumbled to the ground.

"Wish I had some of the Order's lich-killing cantrips," said the fire sprite, as we veered down the street and towards the vampires' place. "That'd teach them."

The sound of a commotion came from within the council house, and I quickened my pace until we reached the door. Within the entryway, two vampires fought hand to hand with a lone spirit mage, using their speed and power to dodge their attacker. I caught up to the mage from behind and grabbed onto his life force one-handed.

When the mage collapsed, I kicked his body aside. More vampires fought with the intruders inside the hallway. Another mage lunged through the vampires' path, bleeding from his shoulder, only to run headlong into Ryan's air magic. The air current ripped through the street, lifting even the liches into the air. Behind them, the Water and Earth Elemental Soldiers ran through the carnage, fighting with swords and magic alike. As I ripped the life force from another lich, a furious-looking vampire threw the mangled body of a dead mage into the street.

"Did they get into the prison?" I asked.

"No," the vampire said shortly. "Two of them escaped underground."

"Earth mages?" Damn. I should have checked Vaughn was definitely dead, but it didn't sound like the enemy had got to Brant. On the other hand, if two of our adversaries had got away, they might have gone through the node.

I headed in that direction and glided to a halt as I spotted someone standing casually against the wall near the node, not bothering to keep himself hidden.

Hawker. His gaze travelled over me, pinning me to the spot. Overflowing with life energy from the liches I'd killed, I had no way to hide my spirit mage status. Nor did I want to.

"Olivia Cartwright," he said. "I should have known it was you. When the Order announced that a spirit mage and a fire sprite escaped their grasp, I realised who I'd had under my eyes the whole time."

"Want a medal, Sherlock?" I said. "You sent your own liches to die, arsehole."

"You seem very much alive," he said. "Despite your antics during your escape from the Order."

"Get fucked." My hands lit up with spirit magic, feeding on the node as well as the lives I'd taken, but he seemed undeterred. He didn't have his usual group of spirit mages acting as his shield, but I had little doubt he had other tricks up his sleeve. He'd nearly killed me once already.

He pushed off from the wall, revealing a cantrip in his hand. I didn't need to see the runes etched onto its surface to know it meant bad news.

"You've certainly been busy," he remarked. "More so than I'd expect from someone who died recently. Twice, am I correct?"

"Three times," I said. "What do you want me to do, thank you for making me more resilient? Because the novelty wore off the second time your mage allies set me on fire."

"Isn't it remarkable?" he said. "I confess I quite enjoyed my afterlife at first. The anonymity was only one perk of being a lich. The immortality was another."

"You're mortal again," I said. "Does that mean your real age will catch up to you?"

"Not at all," he replied. "The reversal spell brought me

back to the age I was when I died. I have a long, full life ahead of me."

"But you aren't planning on sharing, are you?" I said. "The spell is for you alone."

"The spell is for anyone worthy," he corrected.

"And anyone who doesn't take exception to the idea of handing their soul over to the likes of you," I added. "There's nobody I'd trust less with my soul, and anyone with half a brain would agree."

"Ah, but I know you didn't lie to me when you expressed your wish to return to the life you once had," he said. "You were being honest. That is why I'm glad I didn't kill you after all."

"You might want to revise that statement." My hands ignited again, but curiosity tugged at me, demanded to know what his game was. Why had he chosen now to strike against the vampires, and why had he come in person? Had he been hoping I'd show up here?

"I confess I may have been too hasty in deciding to kill you before recruiting you to my team," he said. "In truth, I didn't quite believe Alban's reports of your gift, but it really is quite something."

"Flattery will get you nowhere," I said. "What do you want with the vampires?"

"Nothing whatsoever," he said. "I'm rather more interested in you."

I tensed. "I'm not coming with you."

"You claimed you wanted to join me," he said. "Due to your deep desire to return to life, I assume."

"Yeah, that was before I figured out that you're leading everyone along," I said. "You have no intention of letting anyone use that fancy new spell of yours at all. It's all a lie."

"Not quite," he said. "You were a natural talent as a spirit mage. Unique, in a way. You know how hard it is to learn spirit magic from scratch. Now imagine teaching it to underage mages with the bare minimum of skill. What Dirk Alban did was an uncommon feat, but he chose his apprentice well, and he knew what you wanted, as well as I do. I know you crave power, acceptance, and the freedom to use your magic as you wish."

"You don't know me," I told him. "Not when I was alive, and not now."

"I know what you desire." A smile curled his mouth. "Above your need to return to life, even. Power. Freedom. Having your body back will never be enough."

"I want my *life* back, nothing more," I told him. "And I was willing to work for you in order to get it, if you hadn't decided to insult my intelligence and send me to my death."

"If you'd told me who you really were, then I wouldn't have sent you to die," he said. "I wanted to get rid of the insubordination among my potential recruits. Most of them are pitiful specimens, unworthy to fight at my side. You, however, are exactly what I need, and I'd gladly give you your life back in return for your loyalty."

"No thanks," I said. "You have plenty of spirit mages on your team, but nothing will ever satisfy you, will it? Not until you own the world."

"Then we understand one another, don't we?"

He turned away, and in a flash of light, he was gone.

"Dammit!" I approached the spot where he'd vanished,

but he'd used a trick similar to the Death King, and no traces remained behind.

Incensed, I drifted back towards the gathering crowd as Lord Blackbourne limped out of the council house. His face was bleeding and his expression livid, but at least he was alive—and dragging another vampire behind him.

"This one betrayed us," he said, holding the other vamp by the scruff of his neck. "Let him be an example to all of us."

His fangs flashed and he ripped the vampire's throat out there and then. Arterial blood sprayed out, and in a blur of flesh, the vampire's head rolled to the ground. Lord Blackbourne wiped the back of his mouth with a spidery hand, his eyes bloodshot and angry.

With the smell of fresh blood causing the vampires' pupils to dilate, I found myself glad of my lack of a pulse. I was content to leave them to clean up the mess, but Lord Blackbourne, displaying more self-control than the other vamps, glided over to join me. "Olivia. I wondered if you'd come here."

"What did they want?" I asked. "The liches, I mean? Why'd they break into your home?"

"They stole the video of your trial."

I gaped at him. "What? Why would they want that?"

"For the same reason I showed the video to you, I imagine," he said. "They believe it contains pertinent information."

Damn. The video didn't prove I'd killed Dirk Alban, but did Hawker actually know I'd been the one responsible? Maybe he didn't. He hadn't witnessed anything himself.

I studied the vampire lord. "Does Hawker know

anything about the events which led to my trial? Aside from the public report?"

"I wouldn't know," he said. "I assume his allies in the Order told him what they found when they arrested you."

Me, standing there with blood all over my hands and my mentor dead at my feet. Yet if Hawker had thought I'd killed him, wouldn't he have struck first?

He doesn't know. He thought I was innocent, aside from my recent alliance with the Death King. No wonder he was reconsidering summoning me to his side. If he'd decided I could be coaxed into joining his team, then maybe I could use that to my own advantage somehow.

"The only part on the video was the trial, right?" I asked.

"You just answered your own question," said Lord Blackbourne. "What is left resides in your own mind. Have you remembered yet?"

"No," I said. "Not yet, anyway."

"You promised to tell me what you learned from last night's mission," he reminded me. "I take it the trip to the Order didn't go as promised?"

"Yeah, it turned out not to be an espionage mission after all," I said. "Seems Hawker doesn't like insubordination, so he sent anyone who objected to handing him their soul amulets to get up-close-and-personal with the Order's new lich-destroying cantrips."

"You seem fine," he said.

"I had a narrow escape," I said. "On the plus side, I found out how he killed the other spies."

I'd assumed Hawker was all-knowing, but instead it seemed he was reduced to gathering information via indirect means. Like a video, which would tell him absolutely nothing. His contacts in the Order would have already told him everything he wanted to know... except for everything which had passed between Dirk Alban and me in private.

Maybe that was why he wanted me on his team. Why he'd left me alive.

As the vampire lord retreated into the council house, Dex zoomed over to me. "Nothing like setting a few liches on fire to get the tension out of your system."

"If you say so," I said. "I'm beginning to think Hawker has a secret obsession with me."

"What makes you say that?"

"He stole a video of my trial." I floated back towards the node. "That's why he broke into the vampires' place."

"A video?" he said.

"Lord Blackbourne stole a video from the Order," I explained. "It showed me being tried for using spirit magic. No idea how he got his hands on it. He never told me."

"Not too late to go back and ask him," said Dex.

"I can guess." I scanned the street, but Hawker had left no traces of his appearance behind. "I'd better go back before the Death King thinks I died again."

We went through the node, but no sign of Hawker appeared on the other side. He hadn't targeted the Court of the Dead at all.

Instead, he'd wanted a video. Of me. Or more specifically, proof of my actions on the day of my arrest and Dirk Alban's death.

Too bad only one person had those answers. Me.

12

"What did Hawker steal?" Ryan said blankly. "A video?"

"Of my trial," I added. "Yeah, I know. Apparently, he has a secret crush on me."

They pulled a face. "Ugh. Isn't he a million years old?"

"Not quite, but he's older than he looks," I said. "He told me the reversal spell returned him to the age he was when he died, so I assume he'll age as normal now."

I faced the Elemental Soldiers—minus Bria—and the sprites in the break room, along with Trix. Ryan was still grumpy with me over my second death and leaving them alone in the Withered Oak, but the newest shock had momentarily distracted their attention.

Meanwhile, His Deathly Highness had yet to show his face. According to Felicity, he'd gone to meet the vampires while we were on our way back to the castle, and we hadn't crossed paths on the way. To be honest, I'd be happy to put off the next time we spoke, since I still didn't have the faintest idea what to say to him after our most recent encounter. If not for the fact that I was pretty sure liches couldn't hallucinate, I'd have dismissed it as a dream.

Felicity spoke next. "Why risk getting killed by the vampires just to get his hands on a video?"

"Like she said," Dex told her, "the guy's smitten with her."

"That was a joke," I said. "No, he's got it into his head that I have answers he doesn't. He idolised my dead mentor and now it turns out Dirk Alban was training me as his successor, he wants to know what he told me. Too bad even *I* don't remember our last moments."

"You really…" Felicity gave me an uneasy look. "I know this is none of my business, and the Death King trusts you anyway, but you really worked with the guy who tried to take over the Order?"

"No," I said. "Not Cobb. We had the same mentor, but I was a student at the academy at the time. All I know is that I ended up with no memories and he ended up dead, so it's safe to say Dirk Alban and I weren't best buddies in the end."

Cal leaned forward. "But you admit you worked with that dude? Alban?"

Ryan shot him a warning look, which Cal ignored. To my relief, the Air Element's attitude to me hadn't changed with my new revelations, though after being cleared of stealing the Death King's soul, I'd have to do a lot worse to end up on their shit list again.

As for the others, I'd passed the point of being able to keep secrets from them. As far as the Death King was concerned, I was his hired Spirit Element, which meant they had to deal with me one way or another.

"Yes," I said to Cal. "Allegedly. I have no memory of that period of my life, thanks to the Order, which means this crap is as much of a surprise to me as it is to everyone else."

"Convenient."

"Cal!" said Felicity. "This is a no-judgement zone, Liv. We've all done shit we're not proud of."

Cal scoffed. "Am I the only person who hasn't forgotten Davies?"

"I know the two of you were friends—" Ryan began.

"Yes, and she was dating *his* friend," Cal interjected. "I'm supposed to sit back and ignore it? That on top of her being apprenticed to this Alban dude?"

"I'm pretty sure I'm not the only person in this room who trusted the wrong person," I said. "The Death King himself made the same mistake."

My patience threatened to give way. Cal might have a point, but none of the Elemental Soldiers had moved here before their master had ascended to his position. They didn't know about the curse, nor how closely my history was interwoven with the Death King's.

"She's right." Felicity nudged Cal. "Drop it, all right?"

Cal sighed. "Yeah, fine. I'm supposed to ignore the fact that our fellow Fire Element is running around doing shit behind the Death King's back, too?"

"Where's Bria, anyway?" I asked.

"She went off somewhere after we chased down those mages from the Withered Oak," said Cal. "We caught a few earth mages and handed them over to the vampires."

"Another one blew himself up with an inferno cantrip. That's what burned the place down." I was ninety-nine percent sure Vaughn was dead, and while part of me wanted to tell Brant, he was hardly my priority at the moment.

"Apparently they were leftovers from the Fire Element contest," said Felicity. "Up to their old tricks."

"Yes," said Cal. "The boss told the rest of us to stay on standby and not get involved. I'm sure he'll be thrilled to see we didn't listen."

"You can't expect us to hear that the mages' hideout is under attack and ignore it," said Ryan. "Same with the vampires, for that matter. I'm wondering if Hawker's real goal was to lure out the Death King."

"What does he do when he's not here?" I asked the others. "Aside from astral project to Earth? I know he can't be visiting the Order anymore. Not now they're turning liches into piles of ashes."

"They wouldn't do that to the Death King," said Felicity, though she didn't sound certain.

"They would if he delivered himself to them," said Ryan. "That's what I keep trying to tell him."

"You did?" I turned to them. "You talked to him?"

"Tried," they said. "It was like talking to a brick wall."

"I know that feeling."

Maybe all was not harmonious among the Elemental Soldiers after all. But instead of vindication, I felt more sadness than anything. The Death King was losing control over his army, his territory, and now even the Order had cantrips on their property which could turn his people into dust.

"Yeah, well," said Ryan. "Can't say I didn't try. I reckon he can probably fight the Order's people off if it comes down to it. Provided he doesn't run up against another spirit mage, anyway."

"I think most of them are in the Parallel," I said. "Except Cobb, but he has no magic. He's probably looking for another spirit mage's soul to steal."

"Wouldn't Hawker give him one?" asked Ryan.

"I don't think they like one another much."

Dex snorted. "Yeah, that figures. The problem with these power-crazed menaces is that they don't trust one another, so when shit gets bad, they turn on each other at the drop of a hat."

"I think Hawker's the most dangerous," I said. "He's offering anyone he likes the opportunity to return to life. Never mind that he isn't going to actually give it to most of them, but not many liches would be able to resist the promise."

"Is it just an act, then?" asked Felicity.

"It's false advertising at best," I said. "He had other spirit mages helping him out at first, but they might have been rogues or defectors from the Spirit Agents, not people he helped return to life. Or the criminals he set free from the Order."

It didn't help that the Order had treated murderers the same as innocent mages just trying to exist, so there was no way to gauge how many of the escaped criminals were still a threat. If anyone had done what I had, and learned spirit magic in their free time, they'd have been slapped with a lifelong sentence. My age had spared me from that fate, but if the Order had known I'd killed Dirk Alban, they'd have inflicted a worse punishment on me. Small mercies that nobody knew... except, it seemed, for Lord Blackbourne. I could only assume the Death King was the one who'd told *him,* but that was mere guesswork.

"Do the Order's staff even know their prisoners got

out?" Ryan said. "I know they're unaware of the madman giving them orders, but you'd think they'd have noticed a mass jailbreak."

"Most people aren't allowed in the lower levels," I said. "There weren't many staff in when they led a bunch of liches to their deaths, either."

"Convenient," said Cal. "I think the Order is rotten to the core, personally. I know they outnumber us, but we could easily displace them if we put our minds to it."

"The Death King doesn't want to do that, Cal," Felicity reprimanded. "The liches can't survive on Earth long-term."

True. But the other Elemental Soldiers only knew the basics about the Death King's position. They didn't know the Order held him by the throat, and I still didn't know how exactly they'd implemented their punishment.

I'd bet Hawker did know, but would he really give me that information for free? What about the other liches? Maybe I ought to speak to them myself, but hell if I knew how to convince them to listen to me over their boss. Besides, the last spies had met a horrible end. Even some of Hawker's own supporters had.

Yet he expected me to believe he'd had a change of heart and wanted me alive, as a partner, an equal? Yeah, right. I was better off not setting foot near him again. That's what part of me thought, but a bigger part of me whispered that I was a fool not to take advantage of this opportunity. He might not know the truth, but he'd got me pegged, all right. I'd always wanted something more.

Dirk Alban had known the same. That's how he'd taken me in. Hawker had sounded like my ex-mentor in a manner that disarmed me. I could hardly believe he'd decided to try and recruit me to his team after everything he'd done to my friends, but if Hawker wanted an alliance, then maybe I'd give him what he wanted until I'd pried his means of returning to life from his dead fingertips.

When His Deathly Highness didn't return, I went for a wander around the grounds and found Harper trying to conjure up an illusion of her face.

"It's not working," she muttered, when I approached her.

"Just keep the image in your mind's eye," I said. "Try not to overthink it. Pretend you're human, and you'll trick your mind into forgetting the truth."

"But I'm not." A hand appeared at the end of her sleeve, then disappeared once again. "How the hell does the Death King do it?"

"He's been dead for a decade," I reminded her. "I don't think he's the oldest lich here, either. Have you spoken to any of the others?"

"Do you think I have a death wish?" she said. "Even now I'm like this, anyone in here can rip out my life force and snack on it. Not a nice way to die, that."

"I haven't really talked to the others either," I said. "I'm looking for someone who was turned thirty years ago or more, if you know anyone."

"You mean at the time of the invasion." Her face appeared, and then slid off the hooded mask where her skull was supposed to be. Maybe Devon had a point when she said I'd looked like a melting zombie on my first attempt.

"Yeah." I looked around the castle grounds. "Don't think so hard about the logistics of the illusion. Relax into it. Like slipping on a coat."

She snorted. Then her face reappeared. "More like slipping *off* a coat. We're naked underneath, technically."

"Doesn't really count if there's nothing there," I said. "You're more of a floating head. Better, though. Next you need to work on moving your mouth when you talk."

"Ugh." A sigh came from the place her mouth was supposed to be. "My brother died, you know, and I could have joined him. I almost did."

I frowned. "He died?"

"Yeah... the idiot joined the enemy." She looked down, and her head half-disappeared into her cloak. "He wanted to protect me, and he paid for it with his life."

"I'm sorry," I said. "I don't know if anyone told you, but the liches here... they're under a curse. The entire House of Spirit is. Every one of them turns into a lich. Nobody is spared."

"Damn," she said. "And I thought it was bad enough that I chose this for myself. Is that why they're joining forces with Hawker?"

"They see it as their only way out," I said. "I don't want them to be right, but even if they are, Hawker's plan will backfire on him again. I can guarantee it."

The two of us practised illusions for a bit, until Harper got bored and drifted off. Finding a spot by the window where I could see my reflection, I practised weaving an illusion of my own face. I was getting faster at it, if not a hundred percent accurate. The threads of the illusion came together, and I watched my reflection, practising facial expressions. I shook my head at one of the human skulls in the nearest pillar. "You have more of a range of expressions than I do, mate."

"I wouldn't say that." The Death King approached,

wearing his human disguise for some reason. He reached out and touched my face. "You're improving."

"I—" His finger passed right through my transparent cheekbone with a jolt that zinged through me. "Um. Thanks, I think. Where have you been?"

"Lord Blackbourne has insisted on stationing extra security around the vampires' base," he said. "You took care of the problem fast enough that I didn't see the need to come in person, but he requested the help of some of my liches."

"Good," I said. "But I think he's wasting his time. They already got what they were after."

"The video," he said.

"Yeah, I'm both flattered and weirded out," I said. "He won't get anything useful out of it. I was pretty wiped out by that point. I don't even remember doing the interview."

He was silent for a moment. "Then we'd better hope he doesn't come here next."

"Unless you're hiding any secret videos of me, I think we're safe," I said. "You *aren't*, are you?"

"No."

"Good," I said. "It's bad enough that I have to ask Devon every other week whether or not I rode a unicorn to the prom with Gap-Toothed Dave."

"A unicorn?" he said. "They don't exist."

"I wasn't to know, was I?" I said. "Are you making fun of me?"

Yes, he was. Our eyes met, and I saw amusement glittering there along with some other emotion I couldn't place. Then without another word, he walked into the castle and left me alone outside.

Who was I to you, Greyson Beaumont? I'd asked him.

"Who indeed," I murmured, touching the spot on my face where he'd touched me. The place where, inexplicably, sensation had almost returned. My gaze caught on the window, and my reflection stared back at me, looking as though nothing had changed. As if I hadn't died at all. A lie, but a convincing one.

Dead or alive, I knew what I had to do.

13

Devon took the news as well as I'd expected.

"How many times have you died now?" She shook her head at me across the desk in the shop, where she sat tinkering with a cantrip.

"Three," I admitted. "The last one was Vaughn's fault. He dug a tunnel under the Withered Oak and then blew it up with an inferno cantrip. Then Hawker's liches attacked the vampires, so I had to go sort that out as soon as I woke up."

"Why would they do that?" she said. "To set Brant free?"

"To steal a video of my trial," I said. "I know, I'm disturbed, too. Looks like his obsession with me is worse than I thought."

"I'll watch out in case Hawker's people show up here next and start stealing baby photos of you, then," she said.

"You joke, but it's a genuine possibility," I said. "I have no idea how he even found out Lord Blackbourne had that video. Another vampire must have told him. Or

Brant got in contact with his old friend, but I'm more inclined to blame the vamps."

"Probably," she said. "What did Brant think of all this?"

"No idea, but they didn't set foot near the jail." I shook my head. "On top of that, Hawker showed up and *didn't* try to kill me."

"Really?" she said. "What did he want, then, to exchange phone numbers?"

"To recruit me," I said. "It's bizarre, but I think he's convinced himself that I wanted Dirk Alban to win before I lost my memories. That or he's lying, but you'd think he'd have tried to kill me outright if he thought I was a threat."

As I'd learned already, his power far exceeded mine whether I was a lich or human. Especially when he fought with a group of spirit mages eager to loan him their strength.

"He *did* try to kill you. At the Order." Devon fidgeted with the cantrip, spinning it beneath her finger. "Speaking of which, I've been invited to a conference in London tomorrow night, at their main branch of the Order. They're inviting all the senior staff as well."

"Damn." I stared at her. "What are they doing in London? Is Hawker taking over their Order branch, too?"

"If he hasn't already," she said. "The Order transfers members between branches all the time, not to mention all their long-distance meetings. It's not like the Parallel, where they'd have to meet in person. All they'd have to do was use the phone and recruit people that way."

"This just gets better and better," I said. "So they're spreading across the country. Next it'll be the world."

"Tell me about it," she said. "What if they target the meeting like they did at the reunion?"

"That's one good reason not to go," I said. "You barely got out of there alive, Devon. It's not like I'll be allowed near the place, so I can't help you escape this time around."

"The Death King can," she said. "He's been invited, too."

"Seriously?" I said. "Yeah, I doubt he'll go for that. He knows the Order won't wait to take him out of the picture if they have the opportunity."

"Sure he won't want to see what they're up to?" she said. "If they're meeting at the UK's main branch, it must be major."

"London overlaps with Elysium, doesn't it?" I said. "That can't be coincidental. The citadel there is already the meeting point where Hawker and his team hang out every evening. All they'd need to do was get near a node and they'd be able to bring a whole army into the Order's gathering."

"Shit, you're right," she said. "But… damn. Nobody in the Order will have a clue, because Holland is going around saying everything is fine."

"Meanwhile, there are escaped prisoners on the loose and liches are being herded into the basement to their deaths," I added. "I was going to ask if you'd spoken to Judith French."

"No, I haven't," she said. "Why?"

"When Holland's allies at the Order were chasing me down, she pointed me to the exit and saved my arse," I admitted. "We could use some people in the Order on our side. Once they have London's branch, too, it'll only get harder for us to convince them something's wrong."

"Is there anyone who might be able to alert them to the threat, though?" she said. "Outside the Order, I mean?"

"Maybe the Death King," I said. "If he has any influence left with them. I've no idea."

"Can't hurt to ask him," she said. "How are things with His Deathly Highness at the moment, anyway?"

"Weird," I said. "Really weird."

"Weird how?"

Good question. "I don't know. He still won't tell me how we met. At this point, I have no idea what he has to gain from hiding it."

"Hey, don't ask me," she said. "I know almost everything about him through you. Does it matter how you met? I know you don't remember how *we* met."

"I do," I said. "You invited me to join your D&D group after our exam results came back and we both failed the retakes."

"Just testing you." She smiled, then shook her head. "You knew the Death King before you lost your memories, didn't you?"

"I think we were close to one another," I said quietly. "You wouldn't know that from the way he talks to me now, but I once trusted him to help me kill my mentor. That's pretty major."

"If he knew you before, maybe it was too painful for him to be around you after you lost your memories," she said. "I can't pretend to know what it's like, because I only knew you afterwards, but your mum always said it was tough seeing you forget things that she took for granted that you'd always remember."

A sharp pain pierced the place where my heart had once been. "I didn't know."

"She still loved you," Devon said hastily. "Don't get me wrong. But it's hard to watch a loved one change. Some people can't hack it. My parents couldn't. Once I ran off to join the Order's academy and then failed all my exams, they never got over losing the person they thought I'd be."

"You don't ditch someone you care about." I fought back a sudden surge of anger. "Really, if we were close friends, he might have actually spoken to me afterwards, if just to *tell* me how he felt."

Except he *had* spoken to me, at least once. He'd offered me a cantrip to help me with my exams, and I'd turned him down. And not long after, he'd presumably become King of the Dead. Okay, maybe he did have an excuse for keeping his distance from me.

"It might've felt like talking to a stranger," she said. "I'm not making excuses for him, but I can't even imagine how it felt to lose a close friend and yet have to see them every day."

"He didn't have to see me every day, because he became Death King not long after," I reminded her. "Still, discounting all that, it would be really nice if he'd told me what we did to Dirk Alban."

"Maybe he doesn't know," she said.

"He does," I said. "Lord Blackbourne is the only other person who knows we killed him and even he doesn't know how it all went down. There were no other witnesses."

"Hang on," she said. "I thought that was why the other spirit mages had it in for you. They don't know you killed him?"

"Nah, Hawker doesn't know," I said. "Cobb doesn't either. They both think Dirk Alban and I got caught by the Order by accident. They don't know how he died. In fairness, neither do I."

"Huh?" she said. "What in the world made him hate you so much, then?"

"The fact that I teamed up with the Death King," I replied. "Hawker, Cobb—they all saw it as a personal insult that I chose him over them. Hawker said he's willing to give me a chance anyway, which means his offer to join forces with him might be genuine. Maybe I'm not finished as a spy after all."

Sure would help if I could pull off a convincing disguise as a regular human long enough to make it to the Order's gathering, though. This would be the enemy's chance to spread their influence through the other Order branches, and the further it spread, the harder it would be to undo the damage.

Her forehead crumpled. "Yeah, that's weird. You'd think he would have found out by now."

"The Order doesn't know either," I said. "I mean, I had blood all over my hands when they found me, you'd think they'd draw their own conclusions from that, but the truth's locked up in my memories."

"Which even Hawker doesn't have access to," she added. "That would explain why he resorted to breaking into the vampires' house to steal a video of your trial."

"Hmm." I doubted my memories were the only reason he'd attacked the vampires, but his behaviour genuinely confused the crap out of me. Was he really that convinced I was likely to take his side after all? For all I knew, his real goal was to murder me when my back was turned, but if he'd wanted to unsettle the crap out of me, he'd certainly succeeded.

"Anyway, you should probably tell the Death King about the Order's invitation," she said. "Assuming he isn't already aware."

"I thought he wasn't visiting the Order anymore, but who the hell knows," I said. "Okay, I'll head back. See you in a bit."

Once again, I crossed into the Parallel via the node and landed outside the castle. As I approached the gates, a lich glided up to me.

"Are you Olivia Cartwright?" the lich said.

"Yes." What was going on now? "Who are you?"

"Hawker wants to talk to you," the lich said. "Come to the citadel tonight, alone. I'd advise you not to disappoint him."

The lich vanished from sight before I could reply. Part of me was tempted to chase after him, but Hawker might well rescind the invitation if I killed one of his people, and I'd sworn to find out what he was up to. Now it seemed he did want to meet face to face, this time with full knowledge of my true identity.

Bring it on, then.

14

On the other side of the gates, I spotted the Death King waiting on the steps, a silent dark figure in the gloom. Had he seen Hawker's lich speak to me? I doubted he had, but I slipped through the gates and halted in front of him.

"There you are," I said. "Where have you been?"

"I wasn't aware that you missed me that badly," he said. "I was with Lord Blackbourne, helping him update his security in light of the recent attack."

"Hawker wants to talk to me tonight," I said. "He sent one of his liches to make sure I got the message. Seems he isn't averse to the idea of us becoming allies after all, unless it's another trap."

"Is that so?" he said. "Are you going to say no?"

"I'm going to meet with him, but I might throw his offer back in his face," I said. "For a while, I couldn't figure out why he'd make me the offer in the first place, but I'm not sure he actually knows that you and I killed Dirk

Alban. The reason he hates me is because he thinks I picked you over him, not because I killed his idol."

"So he's offered you a chance to undo that decision?" The Death King's tone was inflectionless, without a hint of whether he thought I should go or not.

"I highly doubt he'll take my word for it," I replied. "It's not like he has any reason to trust me. Are you going to advise me to stay away from him?"

"Not at all," he said. "He likely has the only means to return you back to life, and if you're willing to take the risk, then by all means, go ahead. If anything, his guard is down at the moment, and you might be able to slip through his defences."

I stared at him for a moment. He *wanted* me to go. Did he want to take advantage of the opportunity to send me to act as a spy, even now?

No. That wasn't it. He was giving up. "Don't you want me to bring the cure back for the other liches?"

"We've been cursed our whole lives," he said. "You, on the other hand, have a second chance to live again. If he's willing to offer it to you, you should take it."

"I—" I didn't even know what to say. "If this goes wrong, then… then I guess this is goodbye."

He said nothing more, and I wished instantly that I could take back my words. But what was I supposed to say? That I wished I could bring the cure to everyone in the Court of the Dead, including him? That I wished I hadn't forgotten everything about my previous life… and everything about us?

I forced my thoughts back to the present as I travelled through the node back to the centre of Arcadia. Then I approached the citadel, spotting a couple of liches hovering outside the door.

"Name?" one of them said in clipped tones.

"It's me."

"Viva," he said. "Or rather, Liv Cartwright."

So Hawker had told them all. No surprise there, really. "Am I allowed in?"

"As my master requests." He moved aside to let me through the door, and I entered the citadel.

When they saw me, the liches inside the room moved to surround me, no longer welcoming. They all knew who I was.

"Now I understand why you didn't trust us with your soul amulet," said the lich from behind me.

"Got that right," I said. "I'm told your boss has a compelling argument for why I should stay a member of your little group."

"Not all of us want you here," said the lich. "We should rip out your soul and feed it to the phantoms."

"Tough," I said. "I'm here anyway. Tell Hawker if you have a problem with me and he'll explain why he decided to give me another chance, because I'm as confused as you are."

"Go upstairs," he said. "He's waiting for you. If you try anything, we'll obliterate you, soul amulet or none."

"Threat noted and accepted." I glided up the spiralling staircase, watching my back as I did so.

I reached the door without being challenged, and nobody waited inside the room on the other side. I moved closer to the machinery at the back, wondering what powered it all. Nothing like electricity back home. Magic ran through the machinery like a node, harnessed for the spirit mages' use.

In a flash, Hawker appeared on the raised platform, haloed in white light. "There you are, Olivia. Come with me."

I approached the platform, and the current of energy pulled me into its embrace. We landed inside another room with iron grey walls on three sides and another bank of machinery at the back. A familiar coldness swept over me. The room almost resembled the one we'd left behind, but not quite.

"Where are we this time?" I asked.

"Would it matter if you knew?"

"Guess not," I said. "But I hardly came here expecting you to treat me as an ally. What do you want?"

"I fear we got off on the wrong foot, Olivia," he said. "Now I see that you're truly Dirk Alban's successor, and even the Order couldn't take away your gift."

"Speaking of the Order, do they know you're pulling the strings?" I floated off the platform, a chill I shouldn't be able to feel piercing my transparent cloak. "Have you told them you're making lich-killing cantrips in their basement yet?"

"The Order makes use of the spirit mages' technologies even now," he said. "Their current incarnation was born from the ashes of the old council, but their origins are not forgotten. Not by those of us who were there."

"I already knew you were involved in the war," I said. "You can't expect me to support someone who saw to the deaths of millions of people."

"Did the Death King tell you I started the war?" he queried. "He had yet to be born when the spirit mages fell, and I rather think he knows as little as you do. Many who survived the conflict spun their own version of the truth. Only some of us remember the reality."

"And now you're back for round two, with a revival of Dirk Alban's power play for good measure." I followed his gaze to the bank of machinery at the back of the room. "I assume Alban never got to this stage, or it'd be more widely known."

"It is thanks to Alban and his allies that I was able to rebuild what was lost," he said. "Most of the mages' transporters survived the war, but it's thanks to Alban's efforts that we were able to bring them back into use again."

"I seem to remember you were hiding among the liches during Alban's attempted coup, rather than helping him," I said. "I'm guessing because you were scared of retribution from the people you killed during the war."

"I joined the liches in order to escape unjust punishment," he corrected. "The curse was nothing to what else the Order would have done to me, as you've no doubt seen for yourself."

"I've also seen your own experiments at the Order's headquarters," I reminded him. "Who's to say you won't use one of those cantrips to destroy me as soon as I turn my back?"

"That's a risk you'll have to take," he said. "You know the Death King might easily do the same. He could rip out your soul and end your second life in a heartbeat."

"What is your problem with him?" I said. "He didn't start the war *or* the curse. He was as much a victim as any other spirit mage born in the aftermath of the conflict."

"The Death King is the reason for the hold the curse has on his fellow liches," he said. "If not for the Death

King, the curse would not exist, and he willingly stepped into the role when his time came, knowing that he'd be enslaving his own people."

"The Order implemented the curse on the House of Spirit," I said to him. "Not the Death King."

"Untrue," he said. "The Order as we know it rose out of the survivors of the war, mostly mages who wanted to punish their own in order to escape retribution themselves. They reformed the Houses of the Elements, and they made a deal with the liches who once lived in the Court of the Dead before the House of Spirit was delegated there."

"Made a deal?" I echoed.

"The last King of the Dead cursed his own people, Olivia," he said. "That is why I despise everything his successor stands for, and every lich with a sense of self-respect would agree with me."

I gaped at him, speechless for a moment. "You can't pin the blame for that on the current Death King. He wasn't even born."

"Yet he knew of the fraught history of his role when he took up the mantle," he said. "He knowingly took his people's lives into his hands. If there were no king, they would still be in possession of their own souls."

"Does that mean you aren't doing the exact same to the liches who serve you?" I said. "Because I seem to remember you asking me to hand over my soul amulet to you."

"To ensure you kept your word, of course."

"Is that how you justify it?" Anger sparked inside me. "You're such a fucking hypocrite, you know that? The Death King isn't blackmailing anyone. They're free to leave. The Order keeps everyone in his Court bound to their soul amulets against their will, but he tries to protect them anyway. You're not out for anyone except for yourself."

The Order might not have enacted the curse, but it made a horrible kind of sense that they'd joined forces with liches to inflict their punishment on the spirit mages. Not that it removed the blame from Hawker. He'd sent his people to their deaths and conspired with traitors within the Order to begin with. Cobb was a murderer and a madman. Holland was a power-hungry bastard.

I would never forgive either of them. I wouldn't forgive Hawker, either, but if he wanted to taunt me by trying to cast blame on the Death King for his people's plight, he was barking up the wrong tree.

"I see I'm too late to undo Greyson's brainwashing, then," said Hawker. "I was going to let you in on the secret of getting your life back, but perhaps I made a mistake in bringing you here."

"Call me sceptical, but I reckon you aren't telling me the whole of the story," I said. "It sounds more like you're taking out your own anger on the Death King because you can't handle the humiliation of spending three decades bound to someone else due to your own cowardice."

"Anyone who takes on leadership of the Court of the Dead takes all the souls within into their hands," he said. "He knew that all along. I realise you are ignorant, of course, and dependent on him yourself."

"And whose fault is that?" My voice rang out in the empty room. "You ripped out my soul with your own hands. You ended my life."

He studied me for a moment. "I hoped I might undo that mistake. I *am* working on a way to reverse the Order's curse, you know. The Death King didn't even try."

"So there's a catch after all, is there?"

"You might say that." He gave a slight smile. "I'll see if I might persuade you to see things my way."

He approached a metal door set in the back wall behind the bank of machinery. I watched him open it, and several liches moved over to him, speaking in low voices. At a word from him, one of them exited the room, and a muffled cry came from behind them.

A human cry.

Two more liches left the room, dragging a limp figure between them. As I watched in confusion, they hauled the man over to the bank of machinery and into a kind of cage hooked up to it.

"What is that?" I said to Hawker. "Or should that be, *who* is that?"

"Patience," he said, as the liches deposited the struggling man inside the cage and closed the barred door. "I will show you this as a gesture of goodwill to prove that I keep my word. Yes, Olivia… I will give you a demonstration, and I will return the life to one individual."

Tension gripped me. There was a catch. There must be. He wouldn't just hand me my life back. Not without asking for a price.

One of the liches left the group and drifted over to the raised platform in the centre of the room. Then Hawker strode over to the machine and slammed his palm on a button.

Inside the cage, the man began to struggle, his cries muffled. As he struggled, the machine's lights grew brighter. My metaphorical heart sank in my chest as the truth hit me. The man was a spirit mage… and his life force was powering the machine.

"What the hell are you doing?" I raised my voice over the incessant humming. "Is he supposed to be one of your allies?"

"He volunteered," he said. "Some spells require a certain amount of magical energy to function. A node is best, but in the absence of any better option…"

The mage screamed, writhing on the floor of the cage. A glow suffused his body, emanating from the cage. Inch by inch, the energy flooded the lich on the platform, and his shadowy form filled out with the shape of a real, living man. He looked at Hawker, his gaze brimming with gratitude.

At the same moment, the mage's body slumped to the floor of the cage, dead.

I, meanwhile, stood rigid with shock. Hawker had demonstrated just what I stood to lose if I tried to get my life back. To regain everything I'd lost, I'd have to pay a price.

The only way for me to come back to life was for someone else to die.

15

The machine powered down, the vibrant lights casting shadows on Hawker's face. The chilling amusement in his eyes brought my anger searing back.

"What the hell was that?" I said. "Did you think watching someone die to save a lich's life might convince me to join your side? I think you're deluded, mate."

"Not at all," he said. "I wanted to remind you that all magic has a cost, so I thought I'd give you a demonstration of the choice you must make. It takes a life to save a life… and a spirit mage must pay the price to save another spirit mage."

Shit. That made a horrible kind of sense. A life for a life. Or re-life, as the case may be. Someone like Hawker, I'd sacrifice in a heartbeat, but I doubted I'd get that lucky. No, another spirit mage would have to pay the price if I wanted to return to life.

"Does that mean you're going to get in there next to

save *my* life?" I said. "Because I don't see any other spirit mages in this room."

"That can easily be arranged," he said. "The Spirit Agents' base is close to Elysium's citadel, as I assume you're already away."

"You're one weird, twisted bastard." I shook my head. "Cobb, I understand. Even Holland, too. They want power via the legal route. But you? Why did you attack the vampires? Did you just want the video that badly? Was it worth it?"

"Yes, and I learned a great deal from the footage of your trial," he said. "You truly don't remember anything about your last hours with Dirk Alban, do you?"

"You weren't even there," I said. "You were in hiding, and you let Alban take the fall so you could stay hidden in the Court of the Dead."

"I was watching the whole time, you know," he said. "The Order had to fall first. The Parallel was trickier, the Death King in particular."

"He wasn't Death King at the time," I said. "Greyson. Right?"

"No." His mouth tugged at the corner. "Your ignorance is touching, Olivia, but you must know I'm the only person willing to give you the answers. All you need to do is accept my offer and I'll assuage your curiosity."

"No, thanks," I said. "I'm not all that keen to kill an innocent person to save my own life, especially when it's you who's urging me to do it."

"You think of me as the villain," he said. "Yet it was you who stood at Dirk Alban's side when he planned to dominate the Parallel. I don't believe that person is gone."

"Is that why you're so obsessed with me?" I said. "I'm not whoever you think I am. I never was, even before I was turned into a lich."

"You're more than a lich, Olivia," he said. "You're a spirit mage, and you have the potential to surpass even the Death King if you're allowed to access the full extent of your strength. You deserve the chance to live out your full lifespan while you do so."

"Wow, I'm flattered." I approached the bank of machinery. "Go on, then. Show me the worst."

He slid a cantrip out of his pocket, then fitted it into a slot on the machine. "I'll need something else from you first." He reached into a second slot parallel to the first and pulled out another disc-shaped object. Not a cantrip, but a soul amulet. Its skull symbol reflected the light, but no life gleamed inside it when he carelessly tossed it aside. "This one is empty now, of course."

"You want my soul." I forced a laugh. "You should have known you were wasting your time after the last time you tried to get me to hand over my amulet to you."

"I can't return you to life without your soul amulet," he said. "Luckily, you can provide that yourself, if you desire."

My gaze travelled over the machinery, my thoughts whirling. Now I looked closer, stacks of gleaming cantrips covered the back panel of the machine behind the rows of buttons and dials.

"Where'd those come from?" I said. "Were they the Crow's? This thing is just a giant cantrip with a bigger battery, isn't it?"

"In a way," he said. "The Crow's downfall was that he hadn't the resources or knowledge of how to revive the spirit mages' technology. We needed to find enough power to bring it back into working order."

"Enough power?" We weren't on top of a node. Where did the energy come from, then? The whole tower seemed to vibrate with a low, resonant hum, buzzing in my veins. Coming from behind the door at the back of the room.

I drifted that way. Hawker didn't stop me, not even when I pushed through the partly open door and stared at the sight within.

Several liches remained inside the room, watching over a large cage engraved with runes and hooked up to the machine on the other side of the wall. And inside the cage...

Sprites. They filled the space behind the cage bars, their magic lighting up in shades of all colours. Fire, water, air, earth. Their power was fuelling the machine.

I spun on Hawker. "What the hell are you doing with them??"

"Oh, you have a bond with your sprite friends, don't you?" he said. "They aren't real people, you know. Don't worry about them."

He's twisted. He and his allies were torturing sprites in order to power the transporters linking up the citadels, and I was willing to bet they also bore the cost of turning a lich back into a human again.

"How many did you sacrifice to bring yourself back to life?" I demanded. "How many living souls paid the price?"

"A fair few," he said. "Any prisoners who refused to join my cause had to be dealt with, for one thing. The sprites, though, they're fine... provided they don't try to escape, that is."

Rage twisted in my guts. "What do you really want from me? Tell me the truth."

The machine's lights ignited again, and the transporter hummed, the raised platform lighting up at the edges.

Hawker shot me a glare. "Who did you invite in here?"

"Nobody." Another noise sounded from the transporter. "Maybe it's broken."

He shoved the door open and addressed the liches inside the small room. "Someone's using the transporter. Shut it off."

"But Hawker—" one of them protested.

"Do it."

As the liches swarmed out of the room and over to the transporter, I glided around them and approached the cage of sprites, trying to figure out how to open it. The cruel bastard. How had he even captured so many sprites?

Movement stirred in the corner of my vision. I turned my head and spotted a dark-coloured sprite lurking outside the cage.

"Hey," I whispered. "Is there a key or something?"

The sprite shook his head. I glanced through the open door, but Hawker was too occupied barking orders at the liches to notice the small figure at my side.

The sprite moved close enough to whisper, "He's lying. Even with your soul amulet, you won't return to life. He plans to use a different cantrip once he has you in that cage."

"What cantrip?" I said. "Are you telling the truth?"

"Why would I need to lie?" he said, despair underlying his voice. "My friends are all in that cage. I can't get them out, but you... maybe you can."

"I can try." I moved closer to the machine, and the door behind me opened fully. Two liches floated back in, closing in on me.

"What are you doing?" one of them asked.

"Freeing your prisoners," I said, more to take their attention off the sprite than anything else. "Your master's lying to you, you know that, right?"

"Come with us." The liches reached for me, and I squirmed free and drifted through the open door. When they closed in behind me, I grabbed one of the liches and yanked out some of his life force.

The second lich reached for me and I pivoted, hovering above the bank of machinery. Two slots gleamed within: one empty, waiting for my soul amulet. The other contained the cantrip Hawker had put in there, the one he'd claimed would return me to life—but the sprite had called him a liar. What kind of cantrip was it, then? I didn't recognise the marks on its edge, but if the sprite was telling the truth, Hawker wanted something else from me.

Hawker's attention snapped onto me. "What are you doing?"

"Your liches tried to manhandle me."

Hawker wasn't fooled, of course. His gaze went to the closed door to the back room. "You can't let them out, so don't try it."

"You seriously thought showing me this twisted setup of yours would convince me you're *not* a complete dickhead?" I glided back to the ground in front of the bank of machinery, near Hawker's mystery cantrip. Whatever it was, I had zero desire to be a lab rat.

More humming came from behind me, and lights spun across the ceiling. Hawker swore. "I told you to turn the blasted thing off."

"We didn't do that," insisted one of the liches.

"Don't look at me." While they argued among themselves, I took the opportunity to drift closer to the machine's side. My hand took several attempts to close around the cantrip, and as it slid free in my grip, the lights brightened. Hawker shouted in fury when several people appeared in the centre of the room.

"Thought you might need a hand," said Ryan.

Felicity and Cal stood alongside them, along with Dex. They'd come to help me out after all.

I one-handedly shoved the cantrip under my cloak and conjured a light to my other hand. "Wanna get in the cage, Hawker?"

"So you choose to spurn me, Olivia?" he said. "Very well."

Magic blasted from Ryan's palms, but Hawker dodged their attack, directing the liches to surround the new arrivals. Hawker's hand slammed on the machine and the touch of a button ignited the transporter again. More liches arrived to join the first group, and the answering hum of the machine brought a horrible scream from the room behind the door.

It's hurting the sprites. Anger swept over me, along with the burning desire to make Hawker pay for this.

The ground trembled as Cal raised his hands, while Ryan's air magic rattled the walls. Felicity shot a ball of water at Hawker, but three liches deflected the blow, forming a circle around their leader. The water hit them with the force of a bullet and broke their formation, yet it had no effect on the machinery. I fired a bolt of spirit magic at the liches in front of the machine, but it made no dent on its surface, either. The liches surged forward, reaching for me with icy, grasping hands.

I met them gladly, ripping two liches' life forces out simultaneously. Then I went for the man himself. "Still hiding, are you, Hawker?"

To no surprise, he deflected my attack, two liches collapsing on each side of him as he drew on their life force. Energy surged from his own palms, and I flew backwards into the wall.

As I caught my balance, he threw a disc-shaped cantrip at me. I didn't need to duck, because it passed right through my feet and clattered to a halt. "Yeah, that's not gonna work."

The Elemental Soldiers fought on against the liches. Ryan's magic pushed one of them into my path, and I drew out the lich's life force. Energy flooded me, and I staggered on the suddenly solid floor, disarmingly unbalanced.

Ryan halted mid-attack, gaping at me. "What the hell, Liv?"

"What?" My voice sounded odd. Higher than usual.

"Look at yourself."

I looked down at my own hand—my own *solid* hand—and my gaze flew wide. "What the fuck?"

A laugh snapped my attention back to Hawker, who stood on the platform in the room's centre. "Enjoy your second life, Olivia... if you can."

The transporter lit up, and he vanished along with what remained of his army.

I stared numbly at the spot where he'd disappeared. He'd gone, and he'd left me… alive.

The Elemental Soldiers turned in my direction, and I became acutely aware that I wore nothing except the semi-transparent dark cloak of a lich, which covered my body but left little to the imagination. The floor was ice cold against my bare feet, while my surroundings looked blurred. I didn't have my glasses or contacts, but that was the least of my problems. I rotated on my heel, disarmed to find my feet on the ground for the first time in weeks, and crouched to pick up the newly blank cantrip Hawker had flung at me. As I straightened upright, Dex zoomed over.

"You're back, Liv!" said Dex.

"Don't get too excited," I said. "I'm pretty sure he hit me with one of those cantrips which finished off the Crow and his minions. You remember?"

"The ones that made their limbs fall off?"

"You've got it." I dropped the blank cantrip, which clattered on the ground beside the other cantrip Hawker had put into the machine. I reached down and picked that one up with one hand, though it hardly mattered what Hawker's plan for me had been now he'd put a ticking bomb inside me.

"You have gotta be kidding." Ryan shook their head. "I'm staying out of the room when you tell the Death King."

Oh, damn. How long did I have? Not long enough, in all likelihood. "Shit."

A flicker of movement stirred as the earth sprite came out of hiding, a small humanoid figure glowing with yellowish light.

"Is that a new sprite?" asked Ryan. "Hawker's?"

"He's not with the enemy," I said. "Hawker has a whole bunch of sprites trapped in a cage back there. We have to get them out."

"You're *dying*, Liv," said Ryan. "Unless the sprites have a cure for your condition—"

"Do you?" I turned to the earth sprite.

"No," said the sprite. "I know nothing about cantrips, but my fellow sprites are still trapped inside that cage. There's no key for the door—I looked."

There must be a way to free them. *Think, Liv.*

"Transporter." Ryan grabbed my arm and dragged me over to the platform. "Don't fight me on this, Liv. We can figure out how to save the sprites later."

Spirit magic already raged in my veins, and light engulfed us the instant we stepped onto the platform, taking us back to Arcadia's citadel. The room on the other side appeared deserted, and was downright freezing cold as a human instead of a lich.

"We dealt with all the other liches we ran into," added Ryan. "Come on. No detours."

"All right." I ran. Not glided, but *ran*, because I had legs and feet again. While my muscles felt stiff and unsteady, my body was in full working order. I descended the stairs to the ground floor, careful not to trip over the sheer cloak that barely covered my skin, still gripping Hawker's cantrip in my hand.

Then I walked out into Arcadia, marvelling at the feel of the cold night air on my face. Invigorating. *Living.* I sure as hell didn't feel like I was slowly dying, but even the Crow hadn't been able to reverse the effects of the cantrips he'd devoted his undead life to making. There must be a way around this one.

Wait. Brant would know. He'd worked with the Crow himself, and if my life was at stake, then he'd spill every last one of his secrets.

I was halfway across the square when Ryan caught me up. "Don't make me carry you back to the castle."

"I need to speak to Brant first," I said. "Look, the vampires' council house is right there. Brant knew the Crow, and the old vamp might have told him how to fix this."

"All right," they said. "Felicity, Cal—go tell the Death King we'll be along in a minute."

"Dex, you too," I told the fire sprite. "No, you can't bitch-slap Brant."

"Spoilsport."

The others left via the node, while Ryan and I continued to walk towards the vampires' council house. I was lucky my eyesight wasn't bad enough that I couldn't see where I was going, though the blurred vision gave me a headache and made it difficult to tell how close I really was to collapsing and falling to bits. I hardly cared that I was probably flashing anyone who got too close, because if I didn't get some answers soon, everyone would get an eyeful of my decomposing corpse.

I found the familiar black-curtained windows and hammered on the door to the vampires' council house. This time, the man himself opened the door.

"Olivia!" said Lord Blackbourne. "You're alive again. Excellent. Very interesting choice in clothing, I have to say."

"Hilarious," I said. "Hawker hit me with the same

cantrip that destroyed the Crow, and I don't have long to live. Know any cures?"

"No," he said. "That's quite an unfortunate turn of events."

"No shit," I said. "Can I speak to Brant?"

"How did I guess the fire mage was involved?" He pursed his lips. "Well, to preserve your life, I'll have to let you have your way. Not you, Air Element. Wait outside."

Ryan voiced a protest, but I was already walking past the vampire lord and into the corridor behind him. Alive but dying. What a bloody paradox.

I had to hold a handful of the cloak's sheer material above my ankles as I ran downstairs to the prison and halted in front of Brant's cell. He leapt to his feet with an exclamation. "Liv, you're—"

"Dying," I interrupted. "If you know a cure for the Crow's death cantrips, now's the time to tell me."

His face crumpled. "You picked up one of those things?"

"Hawker used it on me when I refused to join him," I explained. "I don't know how long I have, but if you know a cure, now would be a spectacular time to tell me."

"I know one thing that works," he said, "but it's temporary. You know those neutralising cantrips that switch off nodes? You've handled one before."

"Seriously?" I said.

"Yeah, they kill all magic they touch," he said. "It'll slow the effects down."

"Where's the nearest one?" I asked. "No excuses. Either I get one or I die."

"I'm sorry," he said, "but they moved everything I had

in my bolt hole. Maybe someone at the Withered Oak knows another hiding place—"

"They burned it down," I said. "Rogue mages set the place on fire."

He swore. "The Crow's place was destroyed, too."

"I know, I was there," I reminded him. "Maybe Devon still has one… or the Death King. Your friend Vaughn didn't drop any hints when he came here?"

"Vaughn was here?" He paled. "No way. He should be—"

"In jail. I know." I hardly gave a toss about the earth mage. "Doesn't matter. He's dead now. Blew himself up with an inferno cantrip."

Brant's face fell. "Liv, tell Lord Blackbourne he has to let me out, and I'll find one of those cantrips for you. I'll go to the market, ask anyone—"

Not happening. "If you don't know where to find one, there's no point in taking the risk."

"Liv, wait—" His words faded into the background as I pelted up the stairs, through the corridor and out of the vampires' council house without stopping, painfully aware of the ticking clock hanging over my head.

I halted outside the doors, where Ryan and the vampire lord stood glaring at one another.

"Any luck?" asked Ryan.

"A little," I said. "Turns out those neutralising cantrips which switch nodes off can stall the effects. Got one handy?"

"I'll ask the Death King."

"Do that," Lord Blackbourne said to Ryan's retreating back as they approached the node. "I'd rather not lose my spy."

"You know, I'm really fed up with dying." I followed after Ryan, leaving the vampire behind. I didn't *feel* any different, but it would all change when bits started rotting and dropping off me. No, thanks.

I needed to get my hands on a neutralising cantrip first.

16

Naturally, I found no signs of the Death King back at the castle. After changing into some of my spare clothes from the bag I'd left in the break room and pocketing the cantrip I'd swiped from Hawker's machine, I headed home to meet Devon. It was late at night, but in true Devon fashion, she was wide awake and working on D&D prep when I walked through the node and appeared in the living room.

When she saw me, Devon leapt up from the sofa with a curse. "Hey!"

"Wait—" I ducked as she flung a cantrip at me. "It's me! Liv!"

"What are you using, an illusion spell?" She grabbed another cantrip from the coffee table. "You can't fool me. I know Liv is a lich."

"Whoa," I said. "You're welcome to check me for illusion spells if you like, but I'm really back. Also, I need my glasses."

She paced around me and looked me up and down.

Then her jaw dropped. "Holy shit, Liv. You're real. You're alive. *How?* Did Hawker bring you back to life?"

"Not exactly," I said. "He used one of the Crow's cantrips on me."

"Oh." She fell back onto the sofa. "Oh, *shit.*"

"I'm not a zombie yet," I added hastily. "But I found out there's a way to slow down the effects, if not stop them. I need one of those cantrips which switched the node off. Sounds like they neutralise all magic."

"Damn," she said. "Really?"

"Yeah," I said. "The problem is, Cobb stole the Order's supplies, and knowing our luck, he gave them straight to Hawker. Unless there are some in the warehouse over in Arcadia, but it'll be a pain in the arse trying to break in now everyone can see me again."

Devon cleared her throat. "Um, is this a good time to tell you I already made my own version of that cantrip?"

I stared at her. "You did what?"

She ran through the door into the shop, darted behind the desk, and began rummaging in a drawer. "Yeah, I tried making my own. It's not as good as the original, I don't think, but it should do for now."

"You're a lifesaver." I ducked into the shop and hugged her, and she yelped. "Hey, you can't catch the zombie plague from hugging me, you know."

"No, you're freezing cold, Liv."

"I did just come back from an extended span as a lich," I reminded her. "The Death King isn't around, so you've just saved my life."

"I aim to please." She handed me a carved cantrip and closed the drawer. "That ought to buy you some time. I'm not sure the warehouses will have any in stock, to tell you the truth. The only time I've ever seen one of these cantrips was when Cobb stole a box of them from the Order."

"Maybe Judith knows what the Order did with the rest of their stash." I flicked the switch on the cantrip's side. "Wait. Doesn't it switch the node off?"

"Oh yeah," she said. "Also…"

I felt for the node's presence, but found nothing, while the humming current of energy which had flooded me when I'd drained the liches had dissipated, leaving me drained and tired. I hadn't just turned off the node… I'd also turned off my spirit magic.

"Fuck," I said.

"Yeah, pretty much," she said. "The plus side is that you can go looking for another node to get yourself back into the Parallel without falling to bits."

"The minus side is that if Hawker is lurking out there, I'm dead." Not that I imagined he'd follow me to Earth. He didn't know or care where I'd gone, not when my life was numbered in hours if not minutes.

"You didn't kill him?"

"Nah, he escaped through the transporter in the citadel after he used his cantrip on me," I said. "He thought he killed me, so why bother sticking around?"

"Dickhead," she said. "What was he even doing in there?"

"Torturing sprites to use as batteries for his machinery." I gave her a brief summary of what I'd seen in the citadel. "Not only that, it turns out the only way for me to come back to life is for another person's life to be sacrificed in exchange. Specifically, a spirit mage."

"Ugh." She pulled a face. "I knew there'd be a downside, but damn. Did you have to get hit by one of those cantrips?"

"Hawker threw it at me when I refused to join him." I reached into my pocket and pulled out another cantrip. "Oh, and I picked this one out of the machine. Hawker was pretending it was a spell that would bring me back to life, but a sprite told me it wasn't. Recognise it?"

"Give it here." She took it from me and turned it over. "Nope… I don't know this one."

"Worth a shot," I said. "Whatever it is, Hawker wanted to trick me into walking into it."

"I'll have a look and see if it matches anything in my guidebook," she said. "Go clean up, Liv. And find your glasses."

"Good call." I ran upstairs to the bathroom and had a quick wash before putting fresh contacts in, wincing at the sting on my eyes and cursing my clumsy underused hands. At least I could see properly now, though now the adrenaline had started to wear off, the absence of my spirit magic left me more vulnerable than I'd been in a long time. I'd left my Parallel bag in the Death King's castle, including my lucky dice, so I'd need to stock up from Devon's cantrip stash if I wanted anything to protect myself with when I travelled back into the Parallel as a newly vulnerable human.

"Hey, at least I can join in the next game," I said to Devon, joining her in the shop as she thumbed through a textbook. She had Hawker's cantrip on the desk next to her as she checked its symbols against the illustrations in the book.

"You can," she said. "You don't need your magic to be able to roll dice."

"Always a bonus," I said. "Might need some new cantrips, though."

"Help yourself from the drawer over there."

I did so, my hands fumbling with the desk drawer. "This is gonna take some adjustment. I'm lucky my limbs still work."

"Hmm." She looked up at me from the textbook. "I still don't know what this cantrip is supposed to be, but that glyph there… it means *memory*."

Memory. "It's a memory spell?"

"I don't know," she said. "You'd have to activate it to know for sure, if you want to take the risk."

"I don't, but I can't use it on myself now I'm like this. It wouldn't work." But I had no access to my magic, and if I let the effects of the neutraliser cantrip wear off, the clock would start ticking again.

"Fair point." Devon turned the page of the textbook. "Since Hawker's the one who wanted to use it on you, I can't argue for its effectiveness, either."

The sharp sound of knocking came from the door. "Expecting visitors?"

"Nope," said Devon. "I'm taking a wild guess it's the Order's people, because they have the shittiest sense of timing."

"Crap." The node was switched off, which gave me zero chance of fighting back *or* escaping.

The door slammed open before either of us could move an inch, and two Order staff members entered the shop. One of them was a tall black man who looked like he was part shifter, and the other was Judith French.

So much for her being on our side.

"Liv Cartwright?" said the guy. "You're supposed to be dead."

"I knew you were harbouring a fugitive," said Judith, jabbing a finger at Devon. "Get them."

The man at her side grabbed a cantrip, and I held up my hands in defence. I should have known her attack of conscience wouldn't last. That or she'd been pressured into hauling us both into the Order's jail.

"I'm not your enemy," I warned. "Also, I'm only half alive, and I'm going to rot and fall to pieces within a day. If you capture me and lock me up, you'll have to deal with the mess. Fair warning."

"You're lying," said Judith. "You've been deceiving us all along by pretending to be dead."

"Believe me, I wish I had," I said. "Hawker killed me. He's a lich—or he was one, anyway. He betrayed the Death King, and his allies have taken over the Order."

"You're lying," Judith said. "Come to the Order and cooperate and maybe they'll show you mercy."

"Are you at least going to tell me what crimes I'm meant to have committed?" I said.

"You broke into the Order at least twice," she said.

"I broke *out* of the Order with your help." To her friend, I added, "She helped me escape when Hawker's allies dragged me to the Order in order to have me killed. Have you seen the cantrips they're making in their basement?"

"Stop talking," Judith said. "I mean it. Mr Holland wants to see you, and if we don't bring you in, it's our necks on the line."

Dammit. She wasn't going to listen. Even if she believed me, she was outnumbered, and the Order had worn her down. Could I really blame her for caving in? Judith liked her life simple, and I'd thoroughly wrecked that just by existing in close proximity to her.

Devon grabbed for a cantrip. "Get out of my shop. Last warning."

"We want Olivia," said her shifter buddy. "*You* can stay here, but if you stop us from taking Olivia with us, we'll have to bring you in, too."

Dammit. If I wound up jailed indefinitely, then the effects of the cantrip would run out within a day, and then I'd permanently expire. Worse, telling the Order that wouldn't make them any more likely to take pity on me. If anything, they'd be glad to have an easy way to be rid of me for good.

"If you expect me to hand over my best friend, you're talking to the wrong person." Devon flung a cantrip at the intruders' feet, freezing them both to the spot. Both of them halted midmotion, Judith's eyes still narrowed in a glare.

"What're we supposed to do with them?" I walked around Judith's back. "The nearest node is down the road."

"I know." She grabbed Judith's arms and tugged her towards the shop's door. "We'll take them into the Parallel."

"Not like we have a choice." I joined her in helping to push the two Order members outside the shop door, propping them up against the wall of the house. Then Devon yanked the keys from the door and locked it behind us. "What are you doing?"

"Buying us time." She set off another paralysing cantrip in front of the two Order guards, and took off at a run, leaving the two of them standing outside the house likes statues.

Still bewildered, I followed her at a jog. "They'll figure out we aren't in there pretty quickly."

"Won us some time, though," she said. "We need to get to the Parallel without being followed."

"I don't know if I can even turn on the node like this," I said breathlessly, way too out of shape to push my newly regenerated body into a sprint.

"I can," said Devon. "Not as well as you, but it should be enough to get us out of here."

We skidded to a halt on top of the nearest node, at which point Devon grabbed my arm. For the first time, the light of the node appeared dull, and I felt more resistance than usual when the world began to spin.

After a long two seconds, we vanished and reappeared in an unfamiliar street between two rows of narrow brick houses.

"Dammit, I didn't mean to bring us here," said Devon. "Where—"

"This way." I ran down the street and around a corner, glad of the years I'd spent walking around Arcadia on the Order's behalf for giving me a decent knowledge of its streets. More annoying was the absence of my ability to glide at twice my regular speed and pass through walls. Devon moved faster than I did now, and the node lit up behind us when we rounded another corner. I recognised Judith's voice, and my heart sank. So much for not being followed.

Devon grabbed a cantrip and threw it in the direction of our pursuers, and the two of us broke into a sprint once again.

"The swampland," I gasped out. "I left my weapons there—*damn,* I haven't missed this part of being human."

I was already exhausted, my limbs protesting at the strenuous run after weeks of being a zombie. I didn't really want to kill Judith or her friend, come to that, yet if I ended up captured before we could get our hands on more cantrips to reverse the effects of the curse, I was a goner. And without my spirit magic, the streets of Arcadia seemed awfully quiet, even with the return of the pounding of my heart and my footsteps slapping on the ground.

Devon and I came to the stretch of open ground near the warehouses, where I ran over to a spindly tree marking the entrance to the swamp, relieved to find my spare cantrips stashed inside it along with some weapons. Now I couldn't drain the life from anyone with a touch, I needed another way to fight.

Fucking Hawker.

By some miracle, Neddie the horse was sniffing around the swamp's edge and cantered over when he spotted me. He lowered his head to let me climb onto his back, but he recoiled when Devon tried to join me.

"Neddie, come on, we're being chased." I pulled Devon up after me, and she clung on with a yelp when the zombie horse tried to buck us off.

Then the two Order guards appeared from between the warehouses, one of them wielding a cantrip. Sensing trouble, Neddie reared back, then sprinted for his life. The two of us hung on by our fingertips as the zombie horse hurtled across the swamp and towards the castle at speed.

He didn't stop there, either.

"Gangway!" I yelled at the two liches guarding the gates. "We can't stop—"

Neddie reared back again, and Devon and I both fell off his back into the mud. I landed on my back, and Devon crashed on top of me, knocking the breath from my lungs.

I lifted my head, seeing the Order guards were still pursuing us. They must have used cantrips for stamina or speed, because they definitely shouldn't have caught up to us that fast. I rolled to my feet, and then the gates parted as the Death King appeared behind us. Relief swept over me, and I dug into my reserves for a last burst of speed before heading through the gates and into the Death King's territory. Devon halted beside me, and we collapsed onto the steps outside the castle.

"Holy shit, that was a close one," she wheezed.

"No kidding," I said, equally breathless.

Dex zipped up to me, and I winced when fiery sparks grazed my newly human face. "What have you done now? Did you switch the node off again?"

"Accidentally," I clarified. "Those magic-neutralising cantrips are the only thing that slows down Hawker's spell."

"I had one," Devon supplied. "Unfortunately, the Order found out Liv is still alive and sent people to arrest us."

"Fuckers," said Dex. "How much time do you have?"

I turned to Devon. "How long did the node stay turned off last time?"

"Dunno," she said. "A day at most. My cantrip probably isn't as strong, because I was working from a template and it was a first attempt. I can make a few more, though, if the Death King has the tools."

"He does," said Ryan, approaching at a stride with their face a mask of annoyance. "Really, Liv? You pissed off the Order again?"

"It's my special talent," I said. "Anyway, it looks like the Death King is tearing them a new one over there."

On the other side of the gate, it actually did sound like he was yelling at them, but maybe I was mistaken. He didn't need to raise his voice to terrify people when he could just *look* at them. My body shook with adrenaline, but gradually my breath returned, while the stitch in my chest eased up a little, allowing me to appreciate the brightness of the dawn sky. The stench of the swamp, I hadn't missed as much. I was also tired and starving, worn down by the sheer upheaval of the past day—yet I didn't have time to rest. Not until I found a permanent solution to my half-dead state, preferably before the Order sent another patrol to arrest me.

A transparent figure zipped fast, and I thought it was Dex until I saw the pale brown flash of earth magic. It was the earth sprite from the citadel. He must have followed the others through the transporter and back to the castle.

"Hey," I said to him. "Do you have a name?"

"Terren," he said. "It was unsafe for me to stay at the citadel, but I wish the others could have come, too."

"Same," I said. "I'm sorry I couldn't save them. That machinery was totally impervious to magic."

"Not to dismiss their plight," said Ryan, "but you have a more pressing issue. Namely, that curse of yours."

"I know." I drew in a breath. "I also feel like I've been hit by a truck."

"But on the plus side, you can join us for gaming night again," added Devon.

"Olivia," said the Death King, striding over to our group. "I need to talk to you. Devon, do you have any more of those cantrips?"

"No," she said. "Not yet, anyway. I can make more, but I had to leave the shop—"

"I have all the tools you might need right here," he said. "Ryan, take her with you to the storeroom."

The Air Element looked as though they might argue, but as the Death King gave them a pointed look, they beckoned to Devon and the pair of them headed into the castle.

I turned to the Death King. "What did you do to Judith and her friend?"

"I told them to leave."

"Alive?"

"Out of necessity." He didn't sound thrilled. "I rather think it would have worsened the situation if I sent them home as liches, but I have little care for the Order. They aren't the ones who did that to you."

"Please don't start," I said. "You're the one who encouraged me to go with Hawker."

"Yes, I did." His words were sharp as glass yet cold as a frozen river. "I should have guessed he'd try a dirty trick like that."

"It's not the only dirty trick he pulled. He also told me... he told me the Death King enacted the curse on your people."

"What?" He looked at me as though he thought I had a screw loose.

"Not you," I added. "Your predecessor. He said the liches were the ones who put the curse on the House of Spirit, not the Order, and the first Death King was elected to keep them in line. He claimed that when you took the position anyway, you were implicitly supporting the curse."

He continued to stare at me. "You walked into Hawker's cantrip because of that?"

"No." I shook my head. "That was an accident. I… you know what, never mind. We'll talk about that later."

"You seem overly optimistic that there'll be a 'later'." And without a word of warning, he fired off a bolt of spirit magic into the air. "Do you actively want to *die?*"

"No!" I folded my arms, my heart lurching against my ribcage at the open display of his anger. "I didn't ask the Order to send their people after me, either. If they'd caught me, they'd have locked me in a cage until my timer ran out and I fell to bits. If you want that, feel free to call them back here and hand me over to them."

"I don't want that," he said. "Olivia, I'm trying to hold together an army formed of individuals with divided loyalties and their own grievances, and you're actively trying to endanger your life when you're the one thing I can't turn my back on."

His words knocked the breath from me, yet my mouth kept speaking regardless.

"Everyone thinks I'm valuable, don't they?" I said. "Hawker wanted me to give him my memories, and you—"

"And I what?" he said. "Olivia, I'd prefer it if you picked a fight with someone other than me."

"I'm not picking a fight," I said. "I think that's you, actually. You know, dying is quite enough without being guilt-tripped on top of it."

"That was not my intention."

No. It wasn't. *You're the one thing I can't turn my back on.* How in hell was I even supposed to reply to that?

And as for what *I* felt? I couldn't put words to it, not yet, but the notion of dying before I found out was more than I could stand.

"Greyson Beaumont," I said. "Can you calm the fuck down for a moment? I'm not going to die. Devon is too much of a genius for that. Anyway, I bet Hawker has a solution inside one of his citadels. Problem is, my magic isn't working, so I might have to borrow a spirit mage to use the transporter. That okay?"

"You," he said, "are quite deranged."

I sank into a sitting position and burst into half-hysterical laughter. I knew I was proving his point, but I couldn't help it. I was alive. *Alive.*

This time, I'd make it count.

17

Devon insisted on dragging me to the break room to eat something, while Ryan fetched me the armoured uniform I'd worn when I'd played security guard during the Fire Element contest. Dressed the part of an Elemental Soldier and with my lucky dice in hand, I almost resembled the old Liv, even if I didn't quite feel like it yet.

There'd be time enough to have an existential crisis later. Within the hour, the Death King had called the Spirit Agents to help us rescue the sprites from their prison in the citadel, but they were less than enthused with my plan. Especially when they found out I was dying.

"What the hell kind of cantrip did you get hit with?" Miles hovered above the node, astral projecting into the Death King's territory. The straw-haired spirit mage had held his usual jokey manner up until I'd revealed my fate.

"A cantrip that brings you back to life, and then makes you rot to pieces from the inside out," I explained. "Don't worry, that only happens if you're already dead when it hits you. Vampires and liches need to watch their backs, but the rest of you will be fine."

"Unless he shuts us in a cage and executes us," added Miles. "Yeah, I don't know about this. You said the transporter is powered by *sprites*?"

"They're stuck in a cage," I said. "It's like the machine is using them as a battery. I have no idea where he got them from."

"Fucker," said Shelley, Miles's second-in-command. "I'm all for busting them out. We know how to get into the citadel, right?"

"I'm pretty sure he'll have planned for it," I said. "But if we turn our backs, who knows what else he might do? That machine of his can bring liches back to life, provided he's willing to sacrifice a life for everyone he revives. Turns out that's what he's doing with the spirit mages he freed from the Order's prison."

Miles pulled a face. "Creep. All right. I'm in."

"Same," said Shelley. "I'll get the others."

The pair of them vanished into the node, while the Elemental Soldiers and liches gathered in front of the castle. I, meanwhile, checked my cantrip stash was ready. I'd need to be careful not to get stabbed or hit by a cantrip now I was a vulnerable human again, but if not for the lingering shakiness in my limbs, I might never have died at all.

Devon approached me, holding the cantrip I'd taken from the citadel's machine. "Hey. Liv. If you want to use the memory spell, now's your chance."

"Only after the anti-magic cantrip deactivates," I

reminded her. "And I'm not sure it *is* a memory spell. I mean, Hawker's the one who wanted to use it on me."

"I double-checked it against the textbook, and I couldn't see any signs of tampering," she said. "This is what he wanted, isn't it? It's why he stole the video. He wants your memories back."

"Yeah, but they won't be any safer inside my head," I said. "Also, if I don't remember the past, he won't be able to torture the truth out of me."

She chewed on her lip. "Okay. It's your choice."

"Considering he put a time limit on my life, he couldn't have wanted them that badly," I added.

Still, I had to wonder what he'd hoped to learn. Did he not know Dirk Alban's plans? Was that why he'd wanted my memories—for the same reason Lord Blackbourne had tried to strike a bargain with me? Hawker didn't know I was the one who'd killed Alban... unless this whole thing was a ruse. Either way, rescuing the sprites had to come first, and if we switched off the transporter between the citadels, it would at least slow down Hawker's plans.

"Guess not," Devon said. "Don't get me wrong, I understand why you don't want to be distracted, but maybe your memories are relevant for a reason."

"I'll use the spell," I promised. "When I'm back here and things have calmed down a bit. I need to have another of your magic-neutralising cantrips at the ready, so I don't fall to bits while I'm using the memory spell, too."

"Fair point," she said. "Good luck, okay?"

She hugged me quickly and returned to the castle. I walked to the gates, where the Spirit Agents congregated outside. Only ten or so had showed up, along with Bria.

When she saw me looking at her, she approached me. "Harper wanted me to ask if you found the cure yet."

"You mean for being dead?" I said. "Yeah, there's a cantrip which technically returns someone to life, but there's a major downside. Right now, Hawker's only using those fake ones."

"Fake ones?" she said.

"They bring you back to life but make you rot from the inside out and fall to bits," I explained. "Trust me, Harper doesn't want that."

"Guess not." She held up a cantrip of her own. "You want a way to destroy the machinery? This shit works. I already blew up one of them."

It would have been nice to know that earlier. "Is that one of those inferno cantrips which amplifies fire magic?"

"You've got it," she said. "If I tell you to move, then I'd get outta the way."

"I'll take your word for it on that."

I didn't think Bria even knew I'd been dead until recently, but it didn't matter either way. We had a plan, our allies were ready, and I was more than happy to throw a wrench in Hawker's world domination scheme.

Dex flew over to me, pursued by the other three sprites. "We're all coming to help."

"You sure?" I said. "You might get caught, too."

"Aria said the Crow had her trapped in a similar cage when we rescued her," said Dex. "I bet they were going to use her for the same purpose as those other sprites."

"Shit, I forgot she was stuck in the Crow's basement," I said. "Okay, you can come, but be careful. I can't watch everyone at once."

He flew over to talk to Bria, while I glanced towards

the castle and saw the Death King descending the steps. He wore his human face, surprisingly, but his lich-like form still towered over me now I was made of flesh and blood once again.

I walked over to meet him. "Are you coming with us?"

I wouldn't have thought he'd leave his castle unattended, though I was no longer certain of anything, given what he'd said to me earlier.

Words that made my heartbeat flutter in my fingertips and my body forget I'd been anything other than alive.

"I am," he said. "I have little doubt there's a trap involved, but I will not be bringing my soul amulet."

"You'd bloody better not," I said. "I don't need to worry about your soul on top of mine. I also don't know how long this magic-neutralising cantrip will last."

"Devon's making a backup. She told me."

She could only go so fast, though. I was living on borrowed time and I knew it. I also knew the Death King still hadn't told me everything. I had yet to address Hawker's claim that the liches had been the ones to enact the curse on the House of Spirit, for instance.

The last King of the Dead cursed his own people, Olivia.

Was now the time for that conversation? No, it wasn't. Not if I wanted to keep my attention on the mission. I had a more important matter to address first, besides.

I drew in a breath. "Greyson?"

His own breath hitched, even though he shouldn't have been able to breathe at all. "Yes?"

"Suppose there is a cure," I said. "One without a downside. Would you take it?"

"For myself?" he said.

"Yes," I said. "I know it's a long shot, but if I managed

to lock Hawker in that cage of his, I'd be more than happy to use *his* life as a sacrifice."

He arched a brow. "It's not wise to base all your plans on an accident. I'll wager he's foreseen that possibility."

"Worth a shot," I said. "You should think about it, though. Hawker and his spirit mage allies would happily sacrifice *our* lives."

"Perhaps," he said. "Even if I were to escape the curse, though, we both know what the Order does to spirit mages. I have nothing left outside of the castle. I lost it all when I succumbed to the curse."

"The Order won't hunt you down," I said, though my argument sounded weak to my own ears.

"Why wouldn't they?" he said. "I'm not legally a citizen of the surface world in any capacity. I came here expecting to spend the rest of my existence in this world. You, though, deserve better. That's why, if only one of us can be saved, it has to be you."

I stared at him, open-mouthed. "What makes you think only one of us will be able to return to life?"

"I can tell you're thinking of doing something foolish," he said. "And I want to make it quite clear that I'll see to it that if either of us has to make the sacrifice, it has to be me."

"I don't…" I didn't know what to say. Did he really believe, after all that had come to light, that I'd let him sacrifice his life? That I didn't think him worthy of returning to life?

Before I could formulate a response, the Death King approached the assembled Elemental Soldiers and Spirit Agents without looking back. "Come with me. We will go in through Arcadia's citadel. Expect an ambush—and expect them to be armed."

The Death King led the way out through the gates and to the node. I walked behind him, armed and ready for battle, but despite the array of cantrips I carried, I was acutely aware of my lack of spirit magic and my lack of the invulnerability inherent in being a lich.

Hawker had better not be there. He wouldn't stay away for long, I was sure, but I needed to take the opportunity to get the sprites out before he came back. For all I knew, the sprites might have overheard something useful from Hawker which might point to a way to cure my half-dead state, or maybe an alternative.

If the Death King was determined that only one of us would be saved, I'd have to prove him wrong.

After we passed through the node and into the town square, we approached Arcadia's citadel as a group. I'd wondered how we'd get in, but the Death King reached the door first and extended a hand. The illusion of his arm passed through the solid surface, and the door sprang open.

"I knew you had a way in." I stepped up behind him.

"We aren't alone." He was still wearing his human face, but his mask returned when we found ourselves faced with a group of liches.

"We have company," Ryan warned the others.

The liches swarmed, and the spirit mages sprinted in to meet them. While Ryan and the other Elemental Soldiers joined in the fray, Cal and Felicity stood outside the doors to bar the liches from getting outside. Ryan took the lead through the room, knocking several liches off the spiralling staircase with quick blasts of air magic.

When the path to the upper floor was clear, I ran up the stairs two at a time. The earth sprite flew alongside me. "I can activate the transporter."

"Good, because my own magic is on the fritz," I said breathlessly. "We'll go in quickly and set the sprites free before anyone else shows up."

When I reached the top of the stairs, I shoved open the door and found two more liches waiting on the other side. I flung a paralysing cantrip between them, while Dex flew overhead and sent sparks of fire bouncing off the rune-covered walls. A shower of flames struck one lich, then the other, eating away at their cloaked figures until they turned to dust.

Ryan and two other spirit mages caught up and entered the room behind me.

"I need one of you to hit the button on the transporter," I said to the spirit mages, hopping onto the platform with the two sprites hovering above my head. "Terren here can get us into the right place."

Miles, Bria and some of the others entered next, crowding around the transporter's platform. When one of the mages hit the button, we vanished in a flash and emerged in the room of the citadel where I'd fought against Hawker.

Hawker wasn't there, but several liches swarmed over to us upon our arrival. Bria fired a jet of flames over my head and incinerated one of them, while Dex led the fight against another and the spirit mages added their own attacks to the melee. A nagging voice in the back of my head told me this was too easy, since no living spirit mages waited to fight us, just liches, and even without my spirit magic, our group made quick work of them.

Where the hell was Hawker? Had he expected me to die before I reached the castle again? Quite possibly. I flung another cantrip at a passing lich, while Dex and Bria threw fireballs among them and Ryan's air magic fanned the flames. The machine's light gleamed, mesmerising as ever. Had it always been powered using living beings? Had there once been another source, or had innocent lives always been the fuel for the spirit mages' creations?

"Which city are we in, anyway?" I asked the earth sprite. "Not Elysium?"

"Nowhere," said the sprite. "There's nothing outside the citadel at all."

That doesn't sound good. That must mean this citadel was in one of the towns or cities which had been totally flattened in the war. Gleaming grey walls surrounded us on either side, reflecting Bria and Dex's flames in a manner which made them resemble bloodstains. Déjà-vu prickled at the back of my memory, but with the path clear, I shoved my way through the door to the small room containing the sprites' cage.

"Is that them?" Miles caught me up, regarding the cage with an expression of distaste. Perhaps Hawker had the key, but I wasn't about to chase him down and find out. Better to do things our way instead.

Bria thumbed a cantrip. "Okay. I'm gonna blow the doors off that thing. Stand back!"

"Hang on!" I backed through the door and shouted a warning to the others, who leapt on the platform and engaged the transporter. I ran, too, knowing first-hand how powerful those cantrips were. Yet under the echoing panic, the sickening certainty that I'd been here before nagged at me. *I've seen this place. A long time ago...*

Bria and Miles slammed the door on the back room as the blast went off. The sound tore at my newly reformed eardrums, echoing off the walls. Bright orange flames bloomed from the doors and the sprites flew free in a torrent of chaos and noise. Sparks followed, bouncing off the ceiling, and the tide of sprites flew through the room towards freedom with glad cries.

The smoke cleared, revealing a bank of wrecked wires and busted metal. The transporter had been caught in the blast, too.

Bria looked at it, her eyes widening. "Oops. Might've overdone it."

"You think?" said Miles, with an eye-roll.

"Dammit," I said.

We'd blown up the transporter, leaving us stranded in the middle of nowhere.

And I had a day at most left before the curse took me.

18

Breathing hard, I straightened upright. Only Bria, Miles and Shelley had been left behind, along with Ryan and me. Even the Death King must have been on the other side of the transporter, doing battle with the liches in Arcadia.

Bria herself wore an expression which suggested she thought I might skewer her on the spot. I couldn't deny I was tempted, but despite our predicament, part of me was curious about the area that Hawker had picked out for his hideout. If it wasn't one of the major cities, then where in the Parallel were we?

"Let's have a look outside," I said to the others. "Might as well see what we're up against."

"Did you go over this plan with the Death King first?" Ryan wanted to know. "Because he'll be pissed with you if you gave him no warning before stranding us in the middle of Elements-know-where."

"Keep your hair on," said Bria. "I bet we're close to a

city. The spirit mages didn't build their citadels in the middle of nowhere."

"And you'd know?" Ryan said.

As the two of them bickered behind me, I led the way out of the door at the front of the room and found a staircase leading down into a circular room with similar décor to the other citadels. The silver sheen of the rune-covered walls gave me an uneasy feeling, and the image of blood-covered metal flashed before my eyes again. *This place...*

Bria reached the front door first and opened it. Grey light filtered in, and I followed her outside.

Unbroken wasteland extended outwards in all directions. Not a single node. Even without my spirit magic, I would have been able to see the brightness against the surrounding scenery, but there weren't even any landmarks except for a number of collapsed buildings and piles of rubble. Not unlike the Death King's home, but without the looming shape of a castle dominating the wasteland. I suspected only phantoms and other dead creatures lived here, nothing more.

I walked further outside to let the others fan out behind me, and we surveyed the abandoned stretch of land we'd walked into.

"What're the odds that we run into Hawker's evil lair out here?" I remarked. "Actually, it kinda looks like the other end of the Court of the Dead, but his territory goes on for miles."

"I can look for signs of civilisation," Bria said. "I'm probably the fastest, unless any of you are up for astral projecting."

"What—" I broke off as she strode into the ruins with

speed far beyond what a regular person was capable of. "How are you doing that?"

"Bria has skills," said Miles, with a grin. "I could technically astral project, but I don't quite trust you not to murder me while I'm standing here unprotected."

"*Me?*" I said. "If I'm pissed off, it's because I literally have less than a day to live. I don't have time for a goddamned sleepover in the arse-end of nowhere."

Miles looked alarmed. "A day to live? Seriously?"

"What part of 'cursed cantrip' do you not understand?" I pushed down my anger, with difficulty. None of us had known what we'd be facing, and I hadn't told Bria or the Spirit Agents how truly screwed I was if I didn't find a cure soon. I found myself wishing I'd brought a cantrip to enhance my speed, but I hadn't realised Hawker had picked a hideout in such a remote area.

"What is this place, anyway?" I looked around at the wasteland, which contained enough half-collapsed shells of buildings to make me suspect it'd once been a town.

"Doubt there's a cantrip cure here," Ryan said darkly. "If we have to walk back home, I can carry you and use my magic to boost my speed."

"Let's save that for a last resort." Ryan's ability to use air magic to quicken their walking pace wouldn't be a fun experience as a passenger, but I'd take that over decaying and falling to bits, thanks. "I'll have a look around. Maybe someone left a car in the ruins or something."

Cars were a rare sight in the Parallel, but before the war, they hadn't been non-existent. I paced around, the bleak landscape giving me the same weird sense of déjà-vu as the interior of the citadel. Had I been here before?

Or was the odd spinning sensation in my head because Devon's cantrip was already running out of power?

I reached into my pouch and retrieved the memory spell she'd given me. I ought to be able to use it when my magic came back, so I might at least get to see my lost memories before I died. Assuming it truly was a memory spell and not some new twisted concoction of Hawker's...

A flash of bright light ignited the air, and the tall shadowy figure of the Death King appeared in front of the citadel.

"Oh, hey, there." I lowered the cantrip in my hand. "Knew you'd come and find me."

He didn't speak. The others had spotted him, too, but he walked over to me as though he hadn't seen them. Brightness surrounded him as he took my arm, his grip startlingly tight. My protest was snatched away on the breeze as the world disappeared.

Darkness descended, then lifted again. I was no longer at the Death King's side, but instead, I stood inside the upper room of the citadel we'd just left behind. The machinery glowed, its buttons flashing, while Dirk Alban held a soul amulet up to the light.

My former mentor wore a smile bright enough to rival the sun.

"Between us, we can do anything," he said. "We can kill death itself."

My heart pounded in my chest. "What do you want me to do?"

"Put this—" He waved the soul amulet into my face— "into there."

My hand closed over the amulet. Neon lights of all colours spun on the machine's metallic grey bank, lighting up around a disc-shaped slot in the side of its surface. Dirk Alban stepped into the cage attached to the side of the machinery, and the barred door closed behind him. I, meanwhile, slid the amulet into the slot he'd indicated. At once, the lights on the machine turned to an icy white colour.

"The power of the Death King—of the entirety of the House of Spirit—will be mine for the taking," he said, his voice echoing off the high walls and ceiling. "Thank you for your help, Olivia."

I reached for the soul amulet, which had already begun to glow—but instead of letting its power continue to flow over to Alban's cage, I grabbed the amulet and caught the life force inside it in my palm.

A sudden bolt of pain rippled through my limbs. Dirk Alban screamed in fury, but the energy of the amulet flooded me, quicker and more intense than I'd anticipated. The power of the Death King came free of the amulet… and flowed inside my own veins.

"No!" Alban burst out of the cage, and several other figures ran into the room. "Stop her!"

At a gesture from Alban, the new arrivals moved in on me. I raised my hands in self-defence, and the energy vibrating in my veins shot from my fingertips, striking out like bolts of lightning and piercing my attackers all at once. Blood painted the walls, splattered my hands and face. The machinery trembled with the impact, the energy in my palms brightening until the whole room glowed— but I couldn't stop. I couldn't let go of the energy current, not when it had nowhere else to go.

"What have you done?" Dirk Alban howled. "Olivia Cartwright, you have doomed us all."

"I've done what I had to do," I told him, the roaring in my ears growing louder. *I can't hold this. I'm going to burn up from the inside out.*

His furious scream rang out as he lunged at me. *"You ruined everything, Olivia."*

My fingertips vibrated with energy, but instead of unleashing it on him, my hand plunged straight through his body and grasped the very essence of him. I wasn't thinking any longer, simply operating on pure instinct—and he needed to be stopped.

More light bloomed around my bloody hands, while the transparent shape of a humanoid figure appeared before my eyes. Dirk Alban looked up at me, his mouth stretched into an expression of horror and anger. My body trembled with the force and I braced my feet on the floor in an effort to avoid falling—to avoid letting that terrible surge of power loose into the room...

Then the door slammed open and someone else ran into the room. Greyson Beaumont, his eyes wide with shock. "Liv, what are you doing?"

I couldn't speak. Alban's ghostly figure hovered above my palms, while the Death King's power ran amok in my veins, rippling through my body until my spirit strained at the seams.

"Let him go," Greyson said, comprehension dawning. "If you don't, the power will burn you up from within."

"I *can't*." The light was bright, too bright. I couldn't move my legs. My body locked to the spot, cold sweat sliding down my back, my heartbeat echoing in odd slow thumps.

Greyson ran to my side. "Liv. Liv, are you okay? Can you hear me?"

I couldn't make a sound. My teeth rattled in my skull, my vision blurring, Alban's ghostly voice shouting something unintelligible.

"Liv!" The door slammed behind Greyson again, and he turned to speak to the person who'd come in. "He's dead. She needs help."

Footsteps rushed into the room, but my vision was too blurred to see the new arrival. Greyson's hands found mine, holding tight. "Hang in there, Liv."

Someone swore softly. "What did she do?"

"She pulled out his soul," said Greyson. "I think she's holding onto the Death King's power, too. Alban killed him, but she stopped him from taking his magic by draining his soul amulet."

"Foolish girl," said the voice. "She can't hold onto all that power at once. Nor can you."

"I have to." His own hands had begun to glow, while the machinery continued to reflect the gleaming lights on the blood-splattered walls. "I'll take Alban first…"

Alban himself had faded to almost nothing, but he remained tethered as Greyson carefully removed his soul from my palms. Even without that added weight upon my spirit, the power rattling around inside me burned a path through my veins, and darkness encroached on the edges of my vision.

"She took on the power of the Death King, too," said the voice. "If you remove it from her and let it fade away, you'll be decried as a traitor and a murderer. You'll be blamed for his death."

"Then that's a risk I'm willing to take."

"She's dying," said the voice. Then it clicked into place. Lord Blackbourne… he was talking to *Lord Blackbourne.*

"You can't save her alone. Not without his strength. It was always your fate, Greyson."

"No!" His despairing cry resonated in my mind, mingling with Alban's furious shouts.

"If you have to die for something, then that is an honourable way to end, is it not?" said Lord Blackbourne. "You'll become Death King and save her life at the same time. If you want her to live, you know what you must do."

Greyson gave a shuddering breath. "I'll do it."

Some of the light dimmed, revealing him holding the former Death King's soul amulet in one hand, his other hand closing over mine. Words built in my throat, screaming for release, but the magic pounding in my blood held me captive. Light flowed from me to the amulet, filling its edges, removing the pressure from my chest.

Yet the fog remained, along with the darkness at the edges of my vision. I could no longer see Alban at all, only Greyson, grimly crouching over me as he held up the now-glowing amulet in his hand…

In a rush of light, the breath returned to my lungs… and Greyson Beaumont dropped dead at my side.

———

My vision faded out, then flickered back to reality. I became aware that I lay on a sofa in a living room set out like the Elemental Soldiers' suites, with leather furniture and mahogany fittings. And beside me, the Death King stood so completely still he might have been a statue.

The memories came back in a rush, and I squeezed my

eyes shut to fight the unexpected tide of emotion. Now I knew what I'd done to stop Alban's power play. How he'd met his end. And why Greyson had been there.

I opened my eyes again, and the Death King stirred at my side. "What was that? Don't scare me like that, Liv."

Liv.

I swallowed hard. "Sorry. When you brought us here, I accidentally set off the cantrip I stole from Hawker earlier."

"Cantrip?" he said. "You didn't mention a cantrip."

"You didn't give me the chance to," I said. "Anyway, I never expected it to work."

"What cantrip was it?" He peered into my eyes. "Olivia?"

We were back to Olivia, were we? I looked straight back at him. "A memory spell. That's what he wanted to use on me when he was pretending to offer to bring me back to life."

Except I hadn't remembered what Hawker wanted me to. Unless he wanted intimate details of Dirk Alban's death and the Death King's ascension, anyway. Oh, and the fact that Dirk Alban had been trying to steal the Death King's power all along.

His voice softened. "What did you see?"

The words stuck in my throat as the true horror of what I'd done dawned on me. I'd been the reason for Greyson's death. The reason he'd become Death King. I might not have caused the curse itself to kick in, but all along, I'd been the one responsible for him taking on the position before his time. He must have been wearing a disguise the whole time when I'd seen him in that memory at the academy. He'd come back to see me.

He'd come back to say goodbye.

Tears stung my eyes. If I'd known…

"I'm sorry, Greyson," I whispered. "I'm so sorry."

"You don't have anything to apologise for," he said, genuine concern in his voice. "Whatever you think—"

"I *killed* you." The words scraped at my throat like glass shards. "You had to take the position from the last Death King because I took his power away from Dirk Alban and nearly died from it. I left you no choice. You knew the others might blame you for his death—but it's all my fault. It always has been."

"It isn't," he insisted. "If anything, it's mine, for the way I mishandled the situation with the former Death King. I gave no details to the other liches about how he met his end or why I took his place."

Tears leaked from my eyes and I couldn't stop them from flowing down my cheeks. "I let Dirk Alban kill him. Then I put my own soul in mortal peril in order to destroy him, and you're the one who paid the price."

"The curse would have claimed me in the end no matter what," he said. "You were placed in an impossible situation. I got there too late."

"Because I never gave you the details." I rubbed my forehead. "I have no idea how much I knew of Alban's plans when I confronted him, but if I'd known he was going after the Death King's soul, I should have warned you."

"What would that have achieved?" he said. "He had help. From Hawker, I'm willing to bet, who was likely the one who stole the former Death King's soul amulet and got it into his hands. Besides, you didn't know I belonged to the House of Spirit, nor about the curse. It wasn't well-known outside of our families. It still isn't."

I wanted to argue, but while my mind brimmed with new memories, there were still gaps left behind. I shifted into a sitting position, suddenly aware of how close the Death King was to where I lay. "Is this your room?"

"Yes," he said. "I needed to be ready to heal your soul if the effects of Hawker's cantrip came on."

"Can you do that?"

"I could have turned you into a lich again," he said. "It might not have worked, but I was prepared to act fast."

"How many times have you saved my life?" I shook my head, my nerves thrumming in my fingertips.

"Almost as many times as you've saved mine," he said. "Though the first time you saved my soul from certain peril, you didn't even know my name."

My breath caught. "Yeah. I... I didn't mean to blame you for keeping your distance from me after I lost my memories. I'm sorry I shot down your offer of help, too."

"Help?" he echoed.

"In the exams, you know."

"I forgot about that," he said. "My own recollection isn't perfect, either. I hoped that in time we might be able to build our friendship anew, but I went about it the wrong way."

"By trying to hire me as your Spirit Element," I said. "But... were we friends?"

He stiffened.

"Or..." I licked my dry lips. "Or were we something else?"

"Both." He lowered his head over mine. "You were the reason I stayed."

I lifted my head and our lips met, for a moment—too brief—and then he glided away, towards the door and out of sight.

I half lay on the sofa, my heart racing fast enough I half feared it might escape my chest, and wiped away a fresh sheen of tears. If I came back to life and not Greyson, he might never walk free again. And while he considered his fate to be inevitable, it didn't have to be that way.

I rose to my feet, determination rising within me. I would help him undo the curse, and I'd undo all the wrongs I'd done, that Dirk Alban had done, until we could start anew for real.

Somehow, I had to believe it was possible.

19

I left the Death King's room and walked down the corridor in search of Devon. Moving around the castle as a human was much more slow-going than being a lich, but I was too dazed from my trip into the past to really take it all in. I finally tracked her down in the break room, sitting on the sofa and carving a cantrip.

"Where were you?" Devon looked up, and then she saw my face. "Shit. You okay?"

"Yeah… I think." My gaze snagged on the cantrip lying on the sofa beside her. "Is that what I think it is?"

"Won you a bit more time." She pressed the cantrip into my palm. "I can't say I know how long it'll last. Did you find no more cantrips hidden in the citadel?"

"No useful ones," I said. "Just the sprites. I think he cleared the place out."

Her brow wrinkled. "Why? Did he forget about the sprites?"

"I have no idea, but I found out something more

important." I sucked in a breath. "Devon... I'm the one who killed the last Death King."

"Wait, what?" She blinked at me. "Hang on. You got your memories back."

"Some of them," I said. "I didn't actually kill him, but I might as well have done. Are the others back? Ryan, too?"

"Yeah, why?" she said.

"I think they'll want to hear this as well," I said. "Let's just say the Death King and Dirk Alban are more connected than I ever thought."

"This I gotta hear." She and I left the break room and we tracked down Ryan, Felicity and Cal in the castle grounds. Bria wasn't around, but the sprites descended on us when they spotted me.

"Oh, good, you're back," said Ryan. "What happened? You collapsed, Devon said."

"I was carrying a memory spell when the Death King transported me back into the castle, and his magic somehow triggered the spell," I explained.

They blinked. "Since when did you have a memory spell?"

"I found it in the citadel when Hawker and I had our standoff," I explained. "I never got the chance to use it before we went to rescue the sprites, but Devon and I weren't certain it wasn't a trap set up by Hawker."

"I was ninety percent certain it was the real deal," Devon supplied. "Go on, tell us what you found out."

I gave the others a summary of the memory I'd seen, including the part where the Death King had given up his life and taken on his dead predecessor's position... who, now I thought about it, must have been the person who'd signed the deal with the Order to enact the curse on the rest of the House of Spirit.

With his death, Greyson had been forced to claim his position, yet in Hawker's eyes, he'd taken it willingly. Okay, Hawker hadn't witnessed Alban's failed power play, but if he'd been the one who'd put the Death King's soul amulet into his hands, he'd been partly to blame. What had he said? *It should have been me.* He wanted to be Death King himself, yet he'd been quick to reprimand Greyson for the same choice. Not that I needed any more proof he was a lying hypocrite.

"Damn," Devon said, when I'd finished speaking. "Dirk Alban killed the last Death King?"

"He didn't tell any of the liches?" I asked. "That's the part I don't get."

"No," said Ryan. "When I first started working here, I got curious and asked some of the other liches how the current Death King rose to power, and they said he showed up out of nowhere after his predecessor died in some kind of an accident. He never gave them the details."

"I heard the same," said Felicity. "No real answers. His predecessor didn't hire Elemental Soldiers, either, so there wasn't anyone living to ask."

Cal grunted in agreement. "I never knew, either."

"I can't imagine the last Death King was very popular with the mages," I said. "Considering he ensured the House of Spirit ended up cursed."

"Holy shit," said Devon. "I thought the Order were the ones who put the curse on the liches."

"They did, but they needed the help of the Death King in order to do it," I explained. "It makes sense. Only a spirit mage can remove someone's soul, right? And the

Order banned spirit magic. By working directly with the survivors from the House of Spirit, they could tie the lives of every lich to their leader, and thanks to the curse, every spirit mage who was alive at the time ended up being forced into an early grave."

"The Spirit Agents weren't around back then," Ryan said. "Right?"

"Nah, they won't have been," I said. "Not before the war, anyway, when spirit magic was legal in both realms. I guess anyone who was born with spirit magic afterwards and didn't belong to the House of Spirit needed somewhere to go, so they banded together. Even the Death King used to live with the Spirit Agents before he fell under the curse."

"Yeah." Devon shot me a concerned look. "Except for people like the Crow, and Cobb, and Hawker, who hid themselves after the war. They didn't fall victim to the curse."

"Hawker did," I reminded her. "The Crow and Cobb were both like me, they were trained by Dirk Alban over on Earth and weren't born as spirit mages. I guess Alban must have been the same, but he and the others always planned to take back the Death King's power and restore the spirit mages to their former glory. That's their endgame."

"They want the Death King's power?" said Devon. "You sure?"

"I'm positive," I said. "The Order and the original King of the Dead cursed the House of Spirit so that every one of them turned into liches, and Dirk Alban saw that as an opportunity for a power grab. He realised the potential that came from one lich having domination over all the others. He never wanted freedom for his fellow spirit mages. He wanted the Death King's power for his own—and with it, total control over every lich in the Parallel. Hawker wants the same thing. Cobb did, too."

For all his righteous proclamations, Hawker's goals had never been about freedom for the other spirit mages. Dirk Alban had lured me in with the exact same lies. He'd always intended to take the Death King's power, not caring that it represented the Order's control over the spirit mages and their retaliation for the lives taken in the war. Power meant more to him than justice did. He wanted to rule, nothing more.

"They'll have to try harder," said Ryan. "They haven't managed to take the Death King's soul yet. And if we get hold of the cure for the curse, the liches will have no reason to stay loyal to Hawker."

"Exactly," said Felicity.

"I'm not sure there is a cure," I admitted. "Not without a massive downside, anyway. Like someone else having to die."

"I'd be more than happy to trade Hawker's life for yours," Ryan said.

"The Death King isn't convinced it's possible," I said. "He seemed to think only one of us would get the chance to live. Any idea why he'd believe that?"

"Huh," said Devon. "You and he had a history that went back years, and he must've felt he owed you. Even though you two were enemies."

"We haven't been enemies for a long while," I said, realising it was true. "I don't think I ever really hated him, not after the soul amulet fiasco when we first met."

"When he locked you in jail," said Devon. "With Ryan's help."

Ryan's face flushed. "Look… I regret it. I bet he does, too, though he'd rather tear off his arm than admit it."

"Guess he didn't feel like he had much of a choice." I'd been a stranger to him when I'd got my hands on his soul. Yet things had changed so rapidly in a short space of time that it left me with almost no capacity to deal with any more surprises. "The question is, where *is* Hawker? He must have one hell of an important reason to leave the citadel unguarded except for a handful of liches. Doesn't look like he's in any of the other citadels either."

"Good point," said Ryan. "He must be busy, otherwise he'd have come after us when we were in Arcadia."

"You'd think he *wanted* us to break in and free the sprites," I said. "That, or he didn't care because he was doing something more important."

Devon spun around. "Ah, crap. The meeting at the Order is tonight."

"The what?" My throat went dry. "You mean the one in London?"

"You've got it," she said. "It's this evening. I dunno if Hawker will be there in person, but he isn't an Order member, and nobody will know who he is. He died when the spirit war ended, right?"

"He went into hiding." My heart sank. "But yes… they won't know his face. Even if they did, it's Mr Holland who's running the show. I forgot about that dickhead, to tell you the truth."

Devon groaned. "You know… the Death King has an invitation to the event, too."

I slapped my forehead. "I never told him, because I was kinda distracted by all this other crap."

"I don't really blame you for that, Liv," she said.

"We'll tell the Death King," said Felicity. "Where is he?"

"He's in his suite," I said, as the Elemental Soldiers approached the doors to the castle.

"Back up a step," said Devon. "You were in his *room?*"

"Seriously?" said Ryan.

"Spare me the interrogation." Heat seared my neck and I cursed my human face for being unable to hide my blush. "I bet Hawker's already in London with his mates. Holland, Cobb… and whoever else they have on their side."

If there was a way to expose Holland's treachery to the Order… but even that wouldn't undo the fact that the Order had sown the seeds of their own demise. If Hawker had brought an entire contingent of spirit mages with him, the Order's people might easily be taken unawares like they'd been at the reunion. *It can't happen. Not again.*

While the Elemental Soldiers went into the castle in search of their boss, I strode away from the castle and towards the gates, seeing a group of liches congregating outside. I moved closer, half-expecting to see Hawker himself, but it was Lord Blackbourne who stood on the other side. I didn't think I'd ever seen him out this early in the day, while the sun was still up.

A fresh wave of anger hit me as he caught my gaze, and I marched over to him. "Thanks for telling me you were there when Dirk Alban died, and Greyson became Death King."

"You're welcome," said the vampire lord.

"Seriously, what the fuck?" I glared at the liches until

they pulled back, leaving me face to face with Lord Black-bourne. "Why ask for my memories if you already knew Alban and his allies wanted the Death King's power? It's always been about the Death King. The Order was secondary to him."

Instead, I'd been the one who'd nearly paid the price for Alban's hunger for power, until Greyson had saved me and given his own life in the process. As the vampire lord knew well, because he'd *been* there.

"That wasn't all I wanted to know," said the vampire.

"Isn't it enough?" I said. "Cobb might have wanted the Death King's soul in order to gain back the power he lost, but Hawker wants more than that. He and his allies want total domination over both realms. Which I might have known a long time ago if you'd told me you were *there* when Dirk Alban tried to claim the former Death King's power."

The vampire lord scowled. "Olivia, I had my reasons for not telling you. You didn't trust Greyson, and besides, it was irrelevant."

"My own history is very much relevant," I said through gritted teeth. "And unless someone can find a permanent fix for the curse I'm currently under, there won't be much more of it."

A shadow fell overhead, heralding the arrival of the Death King. "Lord Blackbourne, to what do I owe the pleasure?"

"I merely wanted to talk to Olivia here."

"You should both know, there's a major meeting at the Order in London in about an hour," I interjected. "Devon said you were invited, Death King, but I forgot to tell you."

"You forgot," he repeated. "What is this meeting, exactly?"

"I'm assuming it has to do with why Hawker is mysteriously absent," I said. "And why he left his tower unguarded. He's in London."

"He is?" said Lord Blackbourne. "I assumed he's responsible for the trouble in Elysium I'm hearing about. It seems the mages are stirring up trouble."

"What mages?" Oh, hell. "Was it the same people who attacked the Withered Oak?"

"I would guess so," he said. "I have to admit I prefer it when they don't come so close to my home, given the effects of those inferno cantrips."

Oh. Shit. Infernos? That could only mean one thing… Hawker was planning on turning the gathering into a massacre. Just like the reunion.

I wheeled on the Death King. "We have to stop him."

"We?" he said. "Olivia, how long do you have until the curse comes into effect again?"

"Devon gave me a new cantrip," I said. "Look, the Order needs to be warned. Lives are at stake. Hawker won't expect us. He probably thinks I've already dropped dead by now."

"That doesn't mean he won't be quick to act when we catch up to him," he said.

"Then we'll have to be quicker," I said. "If we don't do this, a lot of innocent people are going to die, and another Order branch will fall under his control."

I had zero doubt that he'd been planning this for a while. He had countless followers willing to lay down their lives for him without a second's thought. Thanks to the quick take-over of the local branch of the Order, he'd stopped word from getting out about the real cause of the attack on the reunion and now he was preparing to do the exact same again.

"I'll leave you to it, then," said Lord Blackbourne.

The Death King glided out of the gates, blocking the vampire's path before he could leave. "Have you done anything to prepare your people for the possibility of another attack? Because if you don't ensure your own safety, we won't always be here to help you out."

"I'd kindly ask you not to insinuate I'm incapable of protecting my fellow vampires."

They broke into an argument, while I looked away, frustration burning within me. Across the swamp, I spotted Bria approaching the castle, accompanied by two of the Spirit Agents.

I walked out into the swampland to meet her. "Where have you been?"

"Elysium," she said. "I take it you know the Houses of the Elements are under attack?"

"The *Houses?*" I shot a glare at Lord Blackbourne. "You didn't say the Houses of the Elements were under attack. That's a world away from a handful of mages stirring up trouble."

"I'm terribly sorry my report wasn't accurate enough for you."

If I were the Death King, I'd have punched him in the face there and then. "Look—you do realise Elysium overlaps with London, which also happens to be the site of the next Order meeting?"

"The Order?" Bria said. "What's going on with the Order?"

I drew in a breath. I didn't know how much she knew

about the Order's corruption—if she lived in the Parallel, not much, in all likelihood—but we were running out of time, and we needed as many allies as possible. "The Order is under the control of the enemy and we've just found out that Hawker and his allies have access to a major gathering in London. We think he might be planning to seize power by unleashing a massacre."

"Holy shit," she said. "Why would he do that?"

"The Order is the centre of the magical community on Earth," I said. "Plus it's an easy way to cover up a coup. Hawker and his allies already used the same strategy once before."

Behind her, Miles gave a low whistle. "Scumbags. The other Spirit Agents are on their way here."

"Good." I just hoped we weren't already too late.

20

Within minutes, a group of us had assembled in the castle grounds, ready to stop Hawker in his tracks. The tricky part was that the liches wouldn't be able to effectively fight in London, since there was no guarantee the gathering would be close enough to a node for them to stay intact. As a result, the Death King had instructed the Spirit Agents to go in instead, but at a safe enough distance that they wouldn't end up being arrested by the Order. Meanwhile, the Death King himself insisted on attending the gathering and wouldn't take no for an answer.

"My Elemental Soldiers will stay here at the castle," he said. "Yes, that includes you, too, Ryan. Hawker wants my soul amulet, so I won't leave it unattended. Bria will go with the Spirit Agents."

"But—" Ryan began.

"Stay here," I said. "He's right—Hawker wants the Death King's power. And even if not, it's what Cobb wants, and that dude is being suspiciously quiet lately. Trust me, it's for the best."

"Fine," the Air Element ground out. "But I expect you to return promptly or else I'll be there to collect you in person."

"And me?" said Bria. "Whatever happened to us going to Elysium?"

"The nodes are switched off," said the Death King. "Or so I am told. However, it may be that you can use the nodes in London to get into Elysium. Keep your distance from the gathering, and make sure nobody sees you."

The nodes are switched off? Elysium was the least of my concerns, yet it sounded like the enemy had found another use for the neutralising cantrips Cobb had swiped from the Order during his escape. Just bloody perfect.

"The Order will be checking IDs on the door," I told the others. "Only the Death King and I have invitations. The rest of you will have to wait outside."

I didn't technically have an invitation of my own, but I'd borrowed Devon's, and the Order would just have to deal with it. If I ended up saving their lives, then it shouldn't matter whether I was on the guest list or not.

"We're not signing up to get arrested, trust me," said Miles.

"Any sign of trouble and we're out of there," added Bria.

I didn't blame her. The spirit mages knew what they risked by coming to London, after all. But once again, the Death King and I would be on our own while we tried to stop Hawker's latest power grab.

At the Death King's word, our group headed for the

node outside the gates. We walked through and landed on a darkening street in the middle of London, at which point I realised that I wasn't dressed for a party in the slightest.

"Not this again." I groaned. "I guess I'll have to pretend I was on the way back from comic con or something."

"I can help." The Death King extended a hand. A flawless illusion slid over him from head to toe, his cloak and armour covered by a tuxedo which fitted to his tall lean frame. I looked down to see a black dress replaced my own armour, hugging my curves.

My heart gave a jolt. "Whoa. I didn't know you could do that to other people."

"You'll have to stay within a metre of me for me to keep the illusion intact," he said.

"So this is a ploy to stop me running off?" I shot him a grin. "I see what you did there."

"The thought did cross my mind." He walked alongside me to the hotel entryway, as though we were a normal couple attending an event. My brain tripped over the word *couple*. Was that what we'd been? Had we ever had the chance, and would we ever get to try again?

"Where'd you get the dress from?" An uncanny thrill raced down my spine as I caught sight of my reflection in the window, arm in arm with Greyson Beaumont. Yet again, a lie, but one so convincing that nobody gave us a second glance as we walked in.

"You won't remember, but you wore it at the leavers' ball after you graduated from the academy," he said, casually handing both our invitations to the security guards on the door.

I stopped mid-step, and my heeled shoes felt realistic

enough to make me a little concerned about tripping over. "You remembered that far back?"

I hadn't known he'd even attended the academy's ball, much less seen *me* there. Yet that wasn't even in the top five ways in which he'd surprised me in the last day.

"Yes, I did."

My breath caught at the hidden meaning lacing his words. He'd seen me there, yet while I'd been approached by an endless stream of guys out to take advantage of my memory loss to pretend that we'd been dating, he'd never said a word to me.

I gave his hand a squeeze, and even *that* felt real. Illusion or not, I couldn't help but dream, for a moment, as spinning lights folded overhead and a chattering crowd enveloped us, of a world where the image I saw in the window wasn't a lie.

Then the lights dimmed enough for me to see everyone staring at the pair of us, and I abruptly wished the floor would rise and swallow me up. Mortified, I looked away from the gathered Order members, most of whom I didn't know. I'd forgotten everyone would have seen that photo of the two of us together, and while not all of them would make the connection between the Death King and Greyson Beaumont, the odds of us not causing a stir were not looking great. At least the security guards hadn't asked to see our IDs, because this wasn't an official Order-owned building. Which made it all the more dangerous if Hawker got inside.

"Interesting crowd," said the Death King, apparently unperturbed by the attention. "I don't see Holland... or Hawker, either."

"He's got to be here somewhere," I said. "Cobb probably isn't, since people would recognise him, but Hawker will be sniffing around in the shadows somewhere. As for Holland, he's the face of Birmingham's Order branch now."

The dense crowd made it hard to move through without knocking into anyone, and I'd already lost sight of Bria and the Spirit Agents the instant we'd passed through the doors. My respect for the Death King's illusion skills doubled, because he never slipped up once.

"If Hawker's here, he's hiding well," he said. "Not that anyone is paying attention."

"I wasn't a fan of formal events even before people started using them as an opportunity to assassinate Order members and cover up coups," I whispered. "I prefer comic con. To be honest, I think you'd like it, too."

"Comic con?" His brow quirked. "In disguise or out of it?"

"Either," I said. "Ryan walked into one in full armour and people thought it was a costume. If you ask me, you could go in there as Death King and everyone would be cool with it."

A scream rang out, along with a loud bang. I pivoted on my heel, scanning the crowd wildly, but I couldn't see the source of the noise.

"False alarm," the Death King murmured.

I followed his gaze and saw several people had popped a champagne cork in the corner of the dance floor. Annoyance flickered inside me. "Wish there was a mic I could grab to warn everyone to evacuate the place. Problem is, Hawker and his allies might be planning on targeting multiple places at once like last time."

"Bria and the others are keeping an eye out for trouble," he said. "We'll be ready."

"Or not." I came to a halt when Hawker stepped into view, dressed in a suit and with a stiff smile on his face. He stood apart from the crowd, beckoning to me with one hand.

The Death King looked in his direction. Hawker lifted his chin and beckoned again. I took that to mean there'd be consequences if I didn't go and speak to him.

"Wait," said the Death King. "*Olivia.* Don't you even think about—"

I walked forward, aware of my illusion fading around the edges as I moved away from the Death King and towards Hawker. My hands trembled with rage, my palm resting on a knife at my waist. I had a free shot at him, but I'd bet he had allies waiting in the crowd to strike if anyone tried to assassinate their master.

"You freed the sprites, didn't you?" Hawker said to me. "Don't assume I didn't hear of your latest exploits."

"You left them there," I told him. "Anyone would think you wanted me to free them. Unlike some people, I don't believe in using other lives as pawns."

"I don't need the sprites," he said. "Soon I'll have more than enough souls for my need."

"What does that mean?" My heart gave a sickening dive. Was he really going to kill everyone in this room the same way he'd done at the reunion? "If you want the Death King's power so badly, why not target him and not a bunch of innocent practitioners?"

"Innocent?" he said. "They work for the Order."

"You want the Order's power yourself," I hissed. "You

don't want them to disband, you want to stand in their place. Don't pretend you're any better than they are."

"I want to dismantle the Order and then rebuild it from the ground up," he corrected.

"With spirit mages in charge?"

"Obviously," he said. "We have the necessary people ready to take command. It'll be a smooth transfer."

"Aside from the unnecessary deaths," I said. "Besides, spirit mages aren't exactly known for being balanced and fair, given all the wars they've started."

"And you're including yourself in that number?" he said. "You were the last person known to have seen Dirk Alban alive."

My shoulders tensed. I'd always assumed he knew I'd been the one who'd killed him despite my recent uncertainty on that point, but I wondered if this was a test of some kind. "What's your point? The Order covered up everything Alban did. They even covered up the fate of the last King of the Dead."

"And are you positive that's all there was to it?" said Hawker. "You remember everything of that fateful day, do you, thanks to the cantrip you took from my tower?"

"I can guess the rest." Of course he'd guessed I'd used the memory spell he'd left behind. "I notice *you* weren't there, but you wanted to become Death King yourself, didn't you? Dirk Alban died and Greyson stepped in before you had the chance to take his power."

His furious scowl told me I was right. *It should have been me,* he'd said. That suggested Dirk Alban had promised to make him Death King, or he'd assumed the title would go to him, but it seemed to me that Alban had betrayed his ally in his moment of triumph.

The noise quietened down as heads began to turn to the front of the room. I scanned the whispering crowd and recognised Cobb among them, crossing the room with a glazed expression on his face.

"What's he doing?" I whispered.

A gleam of light shone from his hands, the vibrant orange of a leaping flame. *Oh, damn.* He was carrying an inferno cantrip.

"He's too much of an inconvenience," said Hawker. "He also desires the Death King's soul for himself, which makes us enemies. And so…"

Cobb climbed onto the stage and faced the audience. More mutters broke out when Cobb lifted the cantrip high, showing it to the crowd.

Hawker's mouth curled up in a smirk. "What a shame."

I took a step towards the stage, though hell if I knew how I could possibly get the cantrip away from him—then a light flashed, and everyone screamed as a tall shadow fell on Cobb from behind.

The Death King. His hand caught Cobb's arm, preventing him from turning on the cantrip. The two of them vanished in another flash, and I half ran towards them, halting when Hawker's fingers caught my sleeve.

"You didn't think I'd have backups at the ready?" he whispered in my ear.

Several dark-clad figures parted the panicking crowd. Two of them climbed onto the stage. I yanked my sleeve away from Hawker, ready to intervene, but instead of pulling out cantrips, one of them grabbed the abandoned microphone.

"Citizens of London and Elysium," he said. "There's recently been a change in management here in London, due to the Order's mishandling of a certain crisis. Mr Alexander Holland, leader of Birmingham's Order branch, is here to tell you more."

Mr Holland ascended to the stage, smiling blandly at the crowd, and took the mic from the other dude. "I apologise for the disturbance you just witnessed. Mr Cobb was a prisoner of the Order and has been returned to custody."

Like hell.

The crowd's mutterings rose again, and Holland waited for the noise to peter out before continuing to speak. "It is time to address a matter of great importance to the Order. In the years since the war, spirit mages such as Mr Cobb were treated terribly, and his desperation is understandable."

"The spirit mages started the war!" someone shouted out.

"And ended it," said Mr Holland, louder. "They deserve recognition for that, and none more than the man who saw to it personally. The man who signed an arrangement with the Order and the Houses of the Elements."

"And who might that be?" someone said.

"Unfortunately, the man himself cannot be here tonight, but his successor is present," said MrHolland. "Greyson Beaumont. You might have heard his name."

My whole body locked to the spot. Sweat trickled down my spine. At first, I felt confident there'd be no reply, but then heads turned towards the room's corner as the Death King walked into view, as though he'd never left.

What the hell is he doing? He must have slipped back inside at some point, but his illusion was back in place, as unruffled as ever despite the attention on him. I could only assume he'd restrained Cobb before coming back.

"Yes?" the Death King said to Mr Holland, in deceptively calm tones. "What is it you want?"

I tried to approach him, but the crowd moved back and around, clearing a path for the Death King to walk to the stage. Gasps sounded when his disguise flickered around the edges, revealing the lich beneath. He must have burned out half his power by transporting Cobb away from here before he blew the place up.

"I think you're overstating the role of the King of the Dead in your arrangement," Greyson said to Mr Holland. "The former Death King was merely a figurehead."

My heart beat erratically, my pulse pounding. Had he seen this situation coming? Surely not, and yet he'd chosen to come back after ditching Cobb. At my side, Hawker wore an unbearable smirk. I inched my hand into my pocket, but his warning gaze made it quite clear he was watching me and not the Death King and he wouldn't hesitate to act if I struck him.

"What the hell are you playing at?" I hissed at Hawker.

"Watch and see."

"Nevertheless, the former Death King took on the position of total control over the other liches in the Court of the Dead," said Mr Holland. "*My* predecessor signed the agreement, in fact, and I believe now is the time to renegotiate that contract."

"In what way?" said Greyson.

"The Order and the Death King placed a curse upon every former member of the House of Spirit," Holland said, and a murmur of speculation travelled through the crowd. "We believe now is the time to undo the curse and allow your people to live their former lives in peace."

The Death King went silent, as though lost for words. So was I. There had to be a catch. Why bring this out in public? What was his aim?

I dragged my gaze away from the stage and onto Hawker. "You're planning on using those cursed cantrips on everyone? You think they'll go for that?"

"Not at all," he said. "I *do* have another way, you know. Don't forget Alexander Holland now owns an entire Order branch."

"Does it involve killing anyone?" His silence went on for a second too long. I trod forward, and someone shot me a glare when I elbowed them in an attempt to get through the crowd to the stage.

"Does that sound fair?" Mr Holland went on. "Your people will all get their lives back, Greyson. Every lich will be free."

"In exchange for what?" Greyson said. "You could have come to me in private to discuss the matter. It's barely relevant to the Order."

"Yet the spirit mages' sacrifice formed the very foundation of the Order as we know it," Holland said. "You became the scapegoats for every crime they committed."

More muttering broke out. It sounded like a fair few people in the crowd hadn't made the connection between the liches and the spirit mages, or maybe hadn't been in the Parallel enough to have a decent education on the House of Spirit. Our academy lessons sure as hell hadn't covered it.

"Not all of us," said Greyson.

"That's true." Mr Holland pointed straight at me.

"Others learned spirit magic independently, for instance. The Order punished them all the same: both innocents and those who committed terrible crimes. Mass murder, for instance. Personally, I believe the punishment should fit the crime."

My heartbeat quickened. He and Hawker had known all along that I'd killed Dirk Alban… and now the entire room did, too, if they'd realised his implication.

"Mass murder?" Someone pointed at me. "She murdered someone? Who?"

Fuck it. If I was going down, I'd do it in style. I raised my head and spoke into the turbulent crowd. "Dirk Alban, a former Order staff member, who recruited me as a fifteen-year-old student to teach me spirit magic. Unbeknownst to me, he planned to overthrow the Order of the Elements, and to take the Death King's power for himself. When he murdered the former Death King, I stopped him from claiming his power, which ended in his death."

"How noble of you," said Holland. "Taking the law into your own hands. Olivia, there may have been a position for you in the new Order, but I believe your second chance has already passed. Meanwhile, we will be negotiating with Greyson here to rescind the punishment for the war."

Like hell. I tried to push through the crowd, only to find Hawker barring my path. He smiled. "Don't be difficult, Olivia."

Dammit. I didn't have access to my magic, and I had no way to fight my way out of this one. My hands clenched.

A deafening blast went off near the doors. Screaming sounded, rippling among the crowd. At once, the Death

King descended from the stage, parting the panicking crowd as he headed in my direction.

Then a second blast in the corner erupted into an inferno, and once again, the crowd broke apart in chaos. The Death King's firm grip on my arm tugged me towards the door, not that I needed any encouragement, and we joined the tide fleeing the building into the street outside. Cold air battered me, numbing my skin, which fit with the disbelief freezing my insides.

The echoing boom of a third explosion made me quicken my pace, and the pair of us ducked into a side street.

"He did it on purpose," I gasped. "He staged the whole thing, didn't he?"

"Correct." Greyson's voice sounded muffled under the aftermath of the blast. "Now the Order will assume the attack was due to a group of spirit mages I brought here myself."

"The Spirit Agents." I looked up and down the street, but the Spirit Agents and Bria were nowhere to be seen. Considering the latter was a fire mage, I was glad of it.

"I ordered them to run far enough away that they won't be blamed for this," Greyson said. "I was prepared for the worst-case scenario."

"Guess you didn't predict that Holland would pretend to pardon you in front of an audience." I grimaced. "That was Hawker's idea, I bet. He wanted to make it look like we threw his offer back in his face."

"Yes, and he killed those people to create a sense of emergency," he said. "No doubt he intends to use the circumstances to push through measures to consolidate his control over London's Order branches, under the guise of protecting the city."

"Not only that," I said. "What in hell was Hawker talking about? He said he already had enough souls and that's why he didn't care that we freed the sprites. Did he have another collection of souls somewhere that we missed?"

"He does now," Greyson said quietly.

I followed his gaze towards the hotel. The whole building lit up like a beacon, rippling with white light.

He'd turned it into a node.

21

Greyson and I stared at the pillar of light shimmering over the hotel. What had happened to the survivors inside the building?

"Everyone inside it was sacrificed." Nausea choked me and I doubled over. "They're dead."

The surviving guests had scattered around the street, pointing up at the painfully bright pillar in the middle of the city, but I couldn't tell if everyone could see the light emanating from the newly created node.

"Please tell me the ordinary people can't see that," I said to Greyson.

"I doubt it," he responded. "They only saw the blast."

That's bad enough on its own. I trod forward, unable to take my eyes off the pillar-like torrent of light covering the spot where the hotel had once stood. A tall, dark outline appeared within the glowing whiteness. "That's... that's a citadel. Is that where the node links up to?"

Greyson nodded slowly. "Hawker wanted to link the node to the citadel on purpose."

"Because we broke his last power source when we let the sprites loose?" Another wave of nausea seized me, and I fought the urge to gag. "He's a fucking monster."

"Don't forget we only destroyed *one* transporter, not the others," said Greyson. "The other citadels are still in full working order, and now one of them is linked directly to Earth. He always planned to do this."

Crap. He was right. Now Hawker and his allies could bring an army right here into London, and nobody except for us would see them coming.

"We have to get in there." I moved towards the pillar of light.

Greyson caught my arm. "Liv, your spirit magic isn't working."

"I reckon stepping into that portal will kick it into gear," I said. "Wait, where did you put Cobb?"

"I left him for my Elemental Soldiers to deal with," he said. "And I got rid of his inferno cantrip."

"Good, because we have enough enemies to deal with already." I emerged onto the main street, scanning the area for any signs of hidden attackers.

"Wait." Greyson walked alongside me, exasperation underlying his tone. "The Order's survivors might be watching—and besides, if you're right, walking into that node will make you vulnerable once again."

Wish I had another of Devon's neutralising cantrips on me. Regardless, if I didn't try to stop Hawker from bringing an army into London, I'd never forgive myself.

"Greyson." I stiffened as he snagged my arm. "Just trust me."

"You said that once before," he said in a low voice. "And I did."

His words cut through me like a guillotine. "Low blow, Grey. Low blow."

Blinking furious tears from my eyes, I advanced on the node. My head swum as my spirit mage vision showed me both buildings transplanted on top of one another: the hotel and the citadel. Linking a spot which previously had been without a node to one of the most powerful sources of magic in the Parallel couldn't be good for either realm. I had an inkling the portal to the citadel would stay open until the energy from the souls dissipated—if it ever did.

After all, the transporter was fuelled by souls, and he'd killed dozens of people. It wasn't the only use for those machines, though, so perhaps this was what Mr Holland had meant when he'd promised the Death King's people would be able to return to life. If the souls whose life force had been absorbed into the node were used to act as a catalyst to set off one of Hawker's life-returning cantrips, Mr Holland's promise would technically be accurate after all.

Yet even if that had been his intention, this wasn't what Greyson had wanted for himself or for his fellow liches. While some liches wouldn't mourn the deaths of several Order members if it meant getting their own lives back, I had no doubts that Hawker and his allies would find a way to make them pay for it one way or another.

The closer we drew to the pillar of light, the quicker the humming sensation returned to my body. Even though I knew each second brought me closer to death, my body reacted to the node's presence as though I breathed clean air for the first time in years. By the time I reached the hotel's doors, my hands buzzed with latent power. My spirit magic was back.

Light dazzled my eyes as I passed through open space where the hotel doors had been blown off their hinges, and Greyson walked at my side. My senses ignited, amplified by the rush of energy from the node, and at once, I knew with certainty that I would do whatever I could to see to it that he escaped the curse. I might not be able to save everyone, even myself, but I would save Greyson.

The light faded a fraction, and my head stopped spinning as my attention focused on the room surrounding us. The inside of the hotel was no longer there, replaced by the downstairs room of a citadel. Greyson took the lead and crossed the room to the spiralling staircase. His mask was back in place along with his armoured clothing, his gaze roving up and down the walls. "We're in Elysium, I think. That's the closest citadel to London."

"These were the instruments that started the spirit war," I whispered. "The citadels, the nodes… they were right in front of us all along. This is how they did it… and now they can do the same to Earth, too."

The Death King made no response, and we climbed the stairs to the upstairs room. Hawker stood beside the raised platform ahead of us in the centre, with a number of spirit mages and liches surrounding him.

"I wondered if you'd come back to claim our generous offer," Hawker said to the Death King. "Since you're the first to arrive, you'll get to be the first of your Court to return to life."

My heart climbed into my throat, but the Death King spoke first. "I'm honoured. Are you offering your own life in exchange?"

The machine gleamed behind Hawker, brimming with energy from the lives he'd sacrificed in the hotel.

"There's no need for any more sacrifices," said Hawker. "Mr Holland didn't lie to you. We are generously extending our offer to every member of the House of Spirit. Any who come here can have the curse undone, and the Order will do nothing to challenge you."

"At what cost?" I said. "You can't expect the Order to support you after you murdered hundreds of people in front of human witnesses."

"The public cannot see any of this," he said. "Besides, soon the Order as you know it will cease to exist. We will replace it with a new Order, not unlike they did after the last war, and this time we will open it to everyone, ordinary humans included. Spirit mages, too. The curse will lift, and you will be free."

I folded my arms, one hand on my cantrip pouch. "And you're doing this out of the goodness of your heart, are you?"

The Order couldn't go on the way it had before, but there was no way they'd accept the likes of Hawker as their spokesperson. He was a spirit mage and a war criminal to boot. Mr Holland, meanwhile, was nowhere to be seen, but he wasn't a spirit mage, so he'd probably gone back home to his own personal Order branch.

If anyone had survived the attack in London, they'd think the Death King and I were the perpetrators. Hawker was unknown to them, while Mr Holland was a respected member of the upper room who hadn't been seen breaking any laws. If people like him existed in every Order branch, they might easily rewrite the secrecy laws and expose the Parallel to humans who had enough crap of their own to deal with without adding ours on top of it.

"I'm doing this because I strongly dislike losing, and

I've been waiting for this moment for a very long time." Hawker considered the Death King. "Greyson. You took what should have been mine."

"Maybe you should have been there yourself," he responded. "Instead of letting Alban do all the work. I'm not sure he really meant for you to have the last Death King's power, besides. I rather think he wanted it for himself."

"Looked that way to me," I added. "I heard him say so, in fact."

"Lies," spat Hawker.

I arched a brow. "You sure about that? You know, I wondered if you stole that video because you had some weird obsession with me, but now I'm starting to think it was Dirk Alban you were obsessed with."

That, I understood. The dude had charisma coming out of his ears. Back when I'd been his apprentice, he could have told me *I'd* be the next Death King and I might have believed him.

Hawker's face flushed purplish-red. "Alban was the first person to offer any of us our freedom back. Nobody else tried. Yes, including you, Greyson."

"You're perfectly aware that's a lie," he responded. "You witnessed my arrival in the castle as the new Death King yourself. No, I didn't make all my attempts to find a cure public, but I preferred not to give false hope to my fellow liches. I also had no intention of sacrificing innocent lives."

"The Order already has blood on their hands," said Hawker. "As for the video, I simply needed to confirm some details about your trial, Olivia, and ensure the vampires wouldn't stand in my way. They know better than to set foot in any of the citadels now."

As he spoke, the whole room gave a faint tremble, light emanating from the runes carved into the walls.

"You wanted me to confess to murder in front of an audience just then, too," I said. "Haven't made up your mind whether I'll be the face of the new Order or its victim? You didn't manage to kill me in the blast, either, so I'm getting mixed messages here."

"I thought I'd let you choose your own fate," he said. "Which is more than the Order ever gave you, I'll bet."

"Choose my fate?" I echoed disbelievingly. "You hit me with a cursed cantrip."

"And if you choose to join me, I'll gladly erase those effects. You can step into that cage and you'll be back to normal in a heartbeat."

"I think I'll pass." Magic sprang to my hands, straight from the heart of the citadel. "I also think you're a murdering tosspot."

Energy shot from my palms, and the Death King moved in the same instant. Our attacks slammed into Hawker and fizzled out as a shield sprang up around him. Four spirit mages stepped forward, fuelling his strength and deflecting our attacks.

Greyson and I stood back to back as five blasts of energy shot at us from Hawker's side. We both called on our own spirit magic but took the hit dead-on, and our shield shattered to pieces. I threw myself to the side to avoid the impact of another strike, which fizzled out against the wall. The Death King glided out of the way, then returned to my side. Two versus five was hardly fair, even if one of us was the King of the Dead.

"What is this place *made* of?" I gritted out. "How can nothing put a dent in the walls?"

Another bolt of energy shot past my head and forced us to duck once again. Yet the attacks made no more impact on the machinery than they did on the walls. The whole place seemed impervious to magic. We were at a stalemate, all drawing on the same fathomless current of energy to power our attacks.

"You want the Death King's soul that badly?" My next strike slammed into one of the spirit mages, but his shield caused the energy to dissipate without causing any damage.

"I want you to remember Dirk Alban," said Hawker. "That is what I desire, Olivia. I want you to remember who he was."

"I remember him, all right," I said. "He was worse than you are, but you're nothing but a pale imitation."

"I waited for years in the Death King's castle before I saw my chance to claim his soul as Dirk Alban promised me," he said, ignoring my words. "You might have been his planned successor on Earth, but I was always destined to rule the Parallel at his side."

Together, Greyson and I blocked another blast of energy from his spirit mages. We could take them on when we combined our strength, but beating five of them at once seemed an impossible feat.

"Give in, Olivia," said Hawker. "You too, Greyson. If you surrender, I might let you survive this with your soul intact."

He and the other four spirit mages stepped into formation, hands aglow—yet they didn't notice the figure who appeared over Hawker's shoulder, wild-eyed and furious.

Cobb lunged at his former ally, an inferno cantrip in his hand. Hawker stumbled back as the other man tackled him to the ground, while Greyson and I backed out of range of the spirit mages' attacks.

"I thought," I said, "you left him in jail."

"I told Ryan to lock him up," said Greyson. "He must have been more determined to escape than I thought."

Cobb leapt on Hawker with a hoarse cry, and an inferno cantrip ignited and then went out in the same instant. *How did Hawker block that?*

A moment later, one of the other mages screamed as fire engulfed him from head to toe. Hawker had used him as a shield, and the man's life was falling apart before our eyes. Flames ripped through the man's skin, and the other spirit mages watched as he turned into a pile of ashes on the spot.

"Holy shit," I breathed.

Cobb jumped at me next, his hand alight with fire and his eyes dancing with madness.

A raging inferno rippled from Cobb's hands. Before it could make contact with us, I blasted him with spirit magic, my heart lurching as his flames narrowly missed Greyson. The Death King wouldn't die if he caught fire, but if he was forced out of the citadel to regenerate back in his castle, I'd be alone to face Hawker and his army. Either the Spirit Agents had ditched us, or Hawker had done something to ensure nobody else could get into the tower. It wouldn't surprise me if he had.

Greyson caught up to me as Cobb came at us with a knife in his hand. One blast of magic from my palm knocked the knife from his grip, which clattered to a halt on the floor. One of the spirit mages moved to intercept him, but Cobb flung a cantrip at him, engulfing him in fire. The smell of melting flesh and ashes made me gag.

Two spirit mages were down. At this rate, Cobb's madness would kill *all* of us.

Cobb dove for the knife, but Hawker snapped his

fingers and spirit magic burst from his palm, knocking his former ally head over heels across the room. Greyson and I both watched Hawker as he approached his former ally.

"They both want your soul," I muttered to Greyson. "Not sure if I'd find that flattering or just plain awkward."

Greyson didn't laugh at my feeble attempt at humour in the face of dire peril. Our only hope of besting Hawker was using the transporter to get backup, either from Arcadia or from anyone we'd left behind on Earth, so I took advantage of Hawker's distraction to approach the bank of machinery. By now, Cobb had managed to pin down Hawker, but Hawker's flailing hand latched onto Cobb's knife and pressed it to his throat. The ex-spirit mage froze, finally registering the danger to his own life.

"That's enough." Hawker pushed to his feet, his nose bleeding. "After everything I've done for you, is this how you repay me?"

"You've done nothing but hide in the shadows when the rest of us suffered for your crimes," Cobb breathed. "The Death King's soul is *mine*. It's the only way I can have my life back. I won't let you take it."

"You're still under the delusion that you have a choice?" Hawker leaned in, the knife biting into Cobb's neck. "Get in the cage."

"What?"

"Get in." Hawker gestured, and his two remaining spirit mage allies grabbed Cobb's arms from behind, hauling him towards the cage hooked up to the machine. "Your soul is not as valuable as it once was, but perhaps I have a use for you after all."

Cobb screamed in fury as the door slammed on him, sealing him inside the cage. His screaming intensified when the lights on the machinery ignited at Hawker's touch.

I moved towards the transporter, but the two surviving spirit mages barred my path.

"Not so fast, Olivia," said Hawker, over the noise of Cobb's screams. "Let this be an insight into your own fate, should you choose to defy me."

Cobb's screaming abruptly cut out, and his body slumped to the ground as the glow around the machinery brightened. With his death, his life force had been sucked into the machine along with the souls of those Hawker had already sacrificed.

"Stop this," Greyson said. "Are you trying to destroy all that remains of what the spirit mages left behind?"

"Not at all," Hawker said. "This is how the Parallel itself was created, built on the sacrifice of those willing to give their lives so we spirit mages could rise to greatness."

Holy shit. The Parallel had been created by sacrificing innocent lives? I glanced at Greyson, but he wore the mask of a lich once again and I couldn't read his expression.

"Why did you need to go to the trouble of sacrificing lives to make a node of your own?" I said. "There's plenty already available."

"None of them link to the very heart of the spirit mages' power," he said. "To the citadels themselves."

"Still not getting what's in it for you." Not without the Death King's soul, anyway.

As he started to reply, more lights flickered across the machine, and the platform of the transporter lit up around the edges. Then a number of figures appeared in its light, including Bria and her Spirit Agent friends.

Hawker glared at the newcomers. "You weren't supposed to be able to get in."

"You didn't account for all of the Death King's spies," said Harper, her lich form joining the mages. "Some of us figured out how to operate the transporter."

"Damn right," said Bria.

The other Elemental Soldiers followed her, dressed in full armour and prepared to fight. Hawker scanned their group, his eyes narrowed. "I have to admit, I hoped to minimise casualties."

"You massacred a roomful of people, you sick bastard." I stepped into line with the new arrivals, my hands lighting up once again. "You deserve everything you get."

I blasted spirit magic at him. He dodged, only to run headlong into Ryan's air magic. Hawker flew backwards and caught his balance against the bank of machinery, slamming his fist on a button. At once, the platform lit up with another flare of light and deposited a group of spirit mages into the room.

Shit. It seemed we weren't the only ones who had backup. Worse, the spirit mages all glowed brightly from being on top of the node. They were at full power.

Then again, so were we.

A spirit mage grabbed for Ryan's life force, but Cal's earth magic made the floor tremble and knocked the mage flat on his face. As another spirit mage lunged at the Death King, he raised a hand and drew out his life force. Ryan leapt over to defend their master.

"I thought you were supposed to be back at the castle," I said to Ryan.

"Like I'd leave you two to deal with this alone," they responded. "What happened in here?"

"A new node links this place directly to London," I explained. "Not only that, it also links to all the other citadels with a working transporter, and anyone who uses it can get out onto Earth. We have to shut it off."

Bria threw a fireball, which bounced off the wall and hit one of the enemy spirit mages in the back. I set off a paralysing cantrip in a spirit mage's face, giving the Death King the opportunity to bring him down. The Death King and I fought side by side, but it was harder than ever to drain the spirit mages' life force when they were standing on top of a node which gave them an endless source of power. Maybe it was too late to destroy the node linking this place to London, but we couldn't fight indefinitely. Even Hawker couldn't, despite all his allies.

I had to finish him off before his deadly cantrip came into effect again.

I sought out Hawker among the other fighters and ran at him from behind. I tried to grab his life force, but it was like trying to catch smoke in my fingertips.

"You'll have to do better than that, Olivia," he said loudly over the ruckus of the machine's humming and the buzz of magic in the air. The cage had opened at some point during the fight, and Cobb's limp body lay sprawled on the floor, trampled beneath the fighting mages.

Magic sprang to my palms. Hawker was awfully close to that cage, and if I got a good hit in, there was nothing to stop me from turning his own spell against him.

I could sacrifice his life to save Greyson's.

A bolt of spirit energy shot from my palms and hit him square in the chest. Hawker staggered, breathless, against the bank of machinery. Then his fist came down on a button, and a paralysing wave rippled through the room.

My body locked to the spot, limbs freezing mid-motion. Yells came from behind me, but I couldn't turn my head and see if the others were okay. Whatever spell he'd used had paralysed my entire body.

Hawker's mouth twisted into a smirk as he strode up to me—and thrust his hand into my chest to grab my life force.

Not again.

My body remained frozen as I fought with all my being, drawing on the node's power, desperately trying to break the connection—and then, abruptly, he let go, giving me a hard shove. My trembling body crashed to the ground, my limbs shaking uncontrollably as the paralysis held them in its grip.

Fingers grasped the scruff of my neck, hauling me upright. I took in the sight of the others frozen mid-fight —enemies and allies both—except for the Death King.

He glided across the room, straight at Hawker, whose grip broke on my neck. I hit the ground again, tasting blood. Struggling to lift my head, I watched the two of them fight it out, their blasts of energy making my teeth rattle in my skull. The Death King looked utterly inhuman, a shadowy figure glowing at the edges with the light of the node as his fist shot into Hawker's chest and clenched around his life force.

"I won't be turned into one of your dead servants," Hawker screamed, his entire body glowing. "I won't—"

"That's enough."

A cold voice slid through my bones. It wasn't Hawker, or even poor deceased Cobb, but the chill echoing monotone of a lich.

A shadowy figure appeared silhouetted in the light of

the transporter, and Hawker took the opportunity to squirm loose from the Death King's grip. His eyes were bloodshot, his hands shaking. "Sir… I can bring her to you now. There's no need for further delay."

"Her?" I managed to lift my head, but the paralysis still held the rest of my body in its grip. "Who the hell are you?"

While the other fighting mages remained semi-paralysed from the effects of the cantrip, the lich moved freely, beckoning Hawker, who grabbed my shoulders and dragged me over to the platform.

The room spun in a halo of lights, my paralysed body vibrating with the force of the transporter's magic. *Where's he taking us this time?* Who *was* that faceless lich? I'd thought Hawker was the guy running the show, but he'd called the other man *Sir.* Maybe there was someone else as the true figurehead, but I couldn't begin to think who it might be.

The light faded. Hawker held my body upright, facing the dark form of the strange new lich. Nobody else was in the room. I blinked in the dazzling lights, disarmed to find myself in the room of the citadel we'd ended up stuck in before when Bria's cantrip had burned out the transporter. Apparently, Hawker had fixed it, because the place looked as good as new.

Greyson appeared in the machine's light, and the paralysing cantrip's effects loosened enough for me to squirm free of Hawker's grip. I gritted my teeth against the sharp pain as my knees buckled, and shot Greyson a look telling him not to intervene. If he did, Hawker could easily rip out my soul without a second's thought. Why else would he have brought me here?

Hawker didn't bother to restrain me, his mouth twisting into some semblance of a smile. He seemed to disregard Greyson's presence entirely, even as the King of the Dead approached him, masked and furious.

The new lich, meanwhile, glided onto the platform. "Is there enough power in this?"

"There should be," said Hawker. "I killed enough of them to run the transporter for weeks, if not months. It should be enough to bring you back, no problem."

My stomach lurched. Was that the true reason for the lives he'd sacrificed? Who *was* this guy, and why had Hawker risked it all to bring him back from death?

"This is what it's all about?" I looked between them. "You want to bring back this dude? I thought it took only one life to bring someone back."

"Generally," Hawker said. "It depends on how strong the individual is. This lich is stronger than most... and he'd very much like to see you again, Olivia."

He was a spirit mage?

Fear trickled down my spine when the machine turned on. The light intensified until it blurred my vision, and the image of a man appeared transplanted over the floating lich on the platform. A face I knew as well as my own.

"I killed him." My voice was a whisper. "He's dead."

"No," said Hawker. "You came close, but I told you that your memories didn't show the full picture, didn't I?"

"What—" I broke off as the machine's lights illuminated a disc-shaped object in Hawker's hand. A soul amulet.

"It took me a long time to find this," Hawker said. "It was well-hidden, but I should have known that devious

Lord Blackbourne took more of the evidence than he let on."

He took it from the vampires. That was what he'd been after. Not the video of my trial. That was merely a convenient cover for his true reason for breaking into the vampires' council house.

"You had him bound," said Greyson. "After Olivia was forced to let go of his soul, you bound it to an amulet, didn't you? You sneaked into the room after the Order took Olivia into custody and I left for the Court of the Dead."

"Correct, but the vampires had the foresight to steal and hide the amulet immediately afterwards," said Hawker. "Come, Olivia. It's time for you to see your old mentor again."

Then he slid the soul amulet into the slot on the machine's surface.

I cursed and leapt at Hawker, but a piercing light ignited on the platform, several vibrant bolts shooting outwards and knocking me onto my back. Another blast of energy knocked the Death King back, too, and even Hawker had to grip the side of the machine for balance as the light enfolded the shadowy form on the platform. Slowly, it solidified into the semblance of a human form.

A man with glossy dark hair. Pale, smooth skin. Light blue eyes as familiar as my own. I'd recognise him anywhere, even wearing the dark cloak of a lich.

Dirk Alban.

23

Dirk Alban had never died after all. Not permanently. Hawker had bound him to a soul amulet after I'd let him go, and he'd remained in stasis this whole time… waiting for someone to return him to life again.

Dirk Alban stepped off the platform. I looked into the eyes of the man who'd ruined my life and felt dread settle deep in my very core.

"Olivia Cartwright," he said. "So the Order didn't kill you after all?"

He didn't know? He must have been stuck in that soul amulet the whole time, for over ten years, but of course he hadn't been able to see anything that had happened in the interim. He didn't know my memories had gone. He didn't know the Order had caught me and blamed me for his crimes, though he'd probably guessed that would be the outcome if he failed.

"Dirk Alban." I matched his tone. "So *I* didn't kill you after all?"

"You ripped out my soul," he said.

"And you tried to use me to help you claim the Death King's power and take over the Order," I said.

"Am I right in thinking at least some of my plan has finally come to fruition?" He glanced at Hawker. "Well?"

"The Order is ours for the taking," he said. "I have forged a new link between London and Elysium which will enable us to step in with ease. With our contacts, it will be a simple matter to spread our influence worldwide."

"And the Parallel?" said Dirk Alban.

"The citadels are back in working order, despite some setbacks," he responded. "Thanks to the efforts of a group of practitioners and the Order's own knowledge, we know how to fix the machinery and have a considerable supply of both cantrips and volunteers."

"Yet they hid my soul well, evidently," he said. "How long has it been?"

"Ten years."

My heart gave a leap. So it was true... he hadn't known. Admittedly, nobody aside from the vampires had known his soul amulet had survived, though I really should have guessed he'd been prepared to find a way back to life. He'd been playing a long game, and while he might not be familiar with the world he'd come back to, he was smart. And powerful.

As for me? I was still running on borrowed time, and yet the energy coursing through my veins mingled with my racing pulse to convince me I was still very much alive.

And ready to fight my former mentor to the death.

Greyson glanced sideways at me as though he'd sensed

my thoughts. At once, power rushed to my hands and banished the rest of the paralysis rippling through my body. My hands ignited as the node loaned me its strength.

"Go on." I faced Alban. "Do your worst."

Dirk Alban glanced at my hands, his brow furrowing. "You think I want you dead?"

"I got you trapped in a soul amulet for a decade," I said. "And I killed at least one of your allies. The Crow."

"Him?" he said. "I assumed he perished already. Cobb, too, though I see I was mistaken about his loyalties."

"Cobb lost his magic when the Order punished him for what you did," I said. "The Order ruined both our lives. You think you can just stride back in here and expect me to welcome you with open arms?"

"Not at all," he said. "I imagine you don't remember our last moments together particularly fondly. Yet you always were my best student, and I understand that you were probably too young to understand what I was trying to do."

"Yeah, no," I said. "I understood perfectly clear, and I still think you're full of shit."

I could hardly believe he was still trying to recruit me even after I'd *killed* him, and after he'd seen to it that I was the one who took the blame for everything he'd done. The Order would have executed him if they'd known he'd survived, but I couldn't believe the soul amulet had remained hidden all this time.

He knew nothing of the suffering the Order had inflicted on those of us he'd left behind, and he didn't yet know I was no longer the girl he'd enticed into giving up her life to join his team. The girl he'd lied to, whose life he'd left in ruins, whose naivety he'd depended on in order to gain her unequivocal trust. That person was gone, lost along with my memories. I'd spent too long mourning her to really think about how glad I was that the man in front of no longer held sway over my choices.

My hands ignited with spirit magic, and I blasted him with everything I had.

Dirk Alban deflected my attack. He wasn't as fast as I remembered, held back by his recent return to life, but his own magic remained intact.

"This is where you died." I caught his life force and tugged, only for him to break away with ease. Bastard.

"You too," he observed. "Until Greyson saved you."

The Death King stepped to my side and the reassuring hum of his own magic bolstered mine. Hawker, meanwhile, joined Dirk Alban. The four of us faced off, then power slammed from our palms, colliding in mid-air. My skin tingled, my teeth rattled in my skull. Maybe I'd faced off against my former mentor before, but I'd never fought him like this, with no holds barred, and in full knowledge of what a twisted power-hungry monster he truly was.

Alban's hand broke through my defences, gripping my life force. Fear splintered me from the inside and I caught his hand in mine, desperately trying to break his grip. If I died here, there was no returning. I'd lose everything again, this time forever.

My gaze hit Greyson's.

I'd lose him, too.

The Death King's magic rippled over me, mingling with mine, and I broke the connection with Alban, shoving him backwards. He caught his balance, his gaze landing on the Death King.

"Greyson, is it? I'm told you're the one who took the position from your predecessor after I killed him."

"Mine isn't the only life you ruined," I told Alban. "You forced him to succumb to the curse the Order inflicted on his family when you killed his predecessor and tried to steal his power."

"I *did* steal his power," he said. "I am more worthy of the position of the King of the Dead."

"I beg to differ." Greyson's hands glowed, and Alban was too slow to deflect the blow. He staggered back, and then Hawker appeared, blasting me off my feet. My back hit the ground, and his hand thrust into my chest, latching onto my life force—

Greyson slammed into him, knocking him head over heels into the bank of machinery. The light of a cantrip ignited, and Hawker howled with manic laughter.

My blood turned to ice when Greyson reeled back, his eyes—his *human* eyes—connecting with mine. He caught his balance against the machinery, his hand gripping the side, his eyes wide, his mouth slack with shock.

Hawker had hit him with a cursed cantrip.

"No!" I screamed, lunging at Hawker. We crashed into one another as I fought to get a grip on his life force. If either of them reached Greyson first, they could kill him before the cursed cantrip had the chance to—but Greyson recovered quicker than I'd expected, his fist striking Hawker in the back of the head.

I set off a paralysing cantrip in Hawker's face, and he fell on top of me. I gripped his life force and tugged, only for Alban to appear behind Greyson. I let go of Hawker and stepped over him to engage my former mentor in battle once again.

Alban studied me over Hawker's frozen body. "You can't win this, Olivia."

Greyson ran to me, but Alban threw a handful of spirit magic at me, sending my back slamming into the bank of machinery. Lights spun around my head, and my spine screamed with pain. I felt blindly for the cantrip pouch at my waist, blood trickling into my eye from a cut on my forehead. Greyson engaged both Alban and Hawker at once, but his newly reformed body was slower than his lich form, unused to fighting with human limitations.

I couldn't watch him die. Either in battle, or when he succumbed to the curse Hawker had inflicted on both of us. And his soul amulet was back in the castle, out of reach.

I struggled upright, wincing as Hawker's magic struck Greyson head-on. My hand closed around a cantrip which lay discarded on the bank of machinery, its faint runes glowing around the edges. The cantrip which had brought Greyson back to life.

At my touch, its surface lit up again—and a realisation crashed over my head. There was no practical difference between the cursed cantrips and the ones which had brought Hawker and Dirk Alban back from death permanently. What mattered was the level of power they had to draw on, and any cantrip that Hawker plugged into the machine had all its reserves of power at the ready, fuelled by the lives they'd sacrificed. Cobb's life force remained inside the machinery, along with the other spirit mages who'd met their end in this very room —not to mention the current of energy flowing from the transporter which linked right up to the newly created node in London.

I had to believe there was enough power still left inside the cantrip to save both of us.

Still gripping it between my fingers, I placed my hands on the machine, and spirit energy poured out from my palms. Alban and Hawker turned my way at once, along with Greyson, whose eyes widened as though wondering what the hell I was doing.

"Hey, dickheads!" I shouted. "Hit me with everything you've got."

As Hawker advanced on me, I astral projected out of my body, zipping to the other side of the machine. I'd had enough practise picking up objects as a lich to reach out and slam my hand down on the button, reconnecting the transporter. Whether there'd be anyone on the other side to come and help us was another matter entirely, but the lights on the platform ignited the instant I touched it. Then I returned to my body, still holding onto the cantrip like a lifeline, as the spirit mages' combined strength hit me with the force of a blow.

I staggered, but Greyson caught my arm before I lost my balance. The whole room trembled as the transporter's lights spun like a fairground ride, a reminder that on the other side of the transporter lay the citadel linked to Earth, overflowing with the power of a hundred lost lives.

"Stop them!" Alban yelled at Hawker, but it was too late. Greyson and I stepped onto the platform, and the light carried us back to Elysium.

Chaos unfolded around us. The battle between the Spirit Agents, Elemental Soldiers and spirit mages raged on, and nobody noticed us at first—the fact that Greyson looked so different as a man didn't help either. I hopped off the platform and waved at Ryan as they sent a spirit mage spinning through the air.

"Liv, what the hell is going on?" Ryan said. "What are you doing—is that the *Death King?*"

"Hawker hit him with a cursed cantrip," I half-shouted. "He'll be through the transporter any second now. Alban, too."

"Did you say *Alban?*"

The transporter lit up and Hawker appeared, knocking spirit mages left and right as he veered around in search of his quarry. His gaze went from me to Greyson, his eyes narrowed. "Stop her!"

Several people descended on me at once, only to find their way blocked by my allies. Hawker tried to grab me, but Greyson blocked his path and gripped his life force in his hand. Hawker snarled in pain, fighting against him.

Then the transporter lit up again, and this time, Dirk Alban appeared on the platform. Magic shot from his palms like bolts of lightning, piercing Greyson through the middle.

"NO!"

My scream tore through the room, and I ran at Alban, only for another bolt of lightning to strike at my feet. Hawker reached for me, but Alban caught his arm from behind, stilling him.

"Enough," said Alban. "Leave them. It's not worth expending any more of our resources on a lost cause. Good luck running your Court now, Greyson."

Hawker ignored him and trod towards the Death King's fallen body, but Alban tightened his grip on his arm. "Calm down, Hawker. He'll be dead within the day. He's nothing. We have places to be."

Hawker shot him a glare, but joined him on the platform. Alban flashed me a smile. "Goodbye, Olivia."

Then he was gone, and so was Hawker.

I ran over to Greyson. He was still breathing, but blood ran from the corner of his mouth and I could see spirals of magic flowing from the jagged tears Alban had left in his soul. His eyes flickered open as he saw me. "What the...?"

I crouched beside him. "Do you trust me?"

His gaze cleared. "Olivia, what are you doing?"

"You first." I hauled his arm over my shoulder and helped him over to the platform. Someone shouted my name, but light swallowed us up an instant later, taking us to the now-vacant room in the other citadel. Operating on pure adrenaline, I dragged Greyson into the cage hooked up to the machine and slammed the door on him. I heard him shouting, heedless of his injuries, but I ignored him and shoved the cantrip in my hand into the slot on the surface of the machine.

The glow brightened as I shoved all the spirit energy I could muster into the cantrip's wake. Greyson exclaimed, his body glowing all over behind the barred door. I could almost see the wounds healing, body and soul, as the cantrip's power and my own life force brought him back from the brink. Was there enough left in there to save the others, too? I didn't know, but I'd done all I could.

As the machine powered down and the last runes vanished from the side of the cantrip, I sank into a sitting position, the light's impression burned into my eyelids. After a few seconds, Greyson kicked down the cage door and walked out, his face incandescent. "Olivia Cartwright."

"You're welcome," I fired back at him.

Greyson stood stock-still, his face pale, a bruise spreading across his cheek. He looked down at his own hands, solid and alive for the first time in over a decade. "I'm—"

"You're alive."

"I'm mortal," he said slowly.

"It's not that bad," I said. "Trust me."

"I doubt the other liches will be very impressed with me," he said. "Look."

I turned to see where he pointed. The lights connecting the cage and the rest of the machinery had died out... and so had the cantrip. I pulled it out with shaking hands, finding both sides wiped clean. Blank.

"Oh, damn." I looked back from the machine to his face. His perfect, very much alive face. "How do you feel?"

"Not like I'm cursed," he said. "But you... you don't look like you are, either."

"How would you know?"

"Like this."

His hand shot through me, grabbing onto my life force. My body stiffened, my mouth falling open, as he let go just as quickly.

"What was that?"

"You feel... whole." He lowered his hand. "I think you healed the effects of the cursed cantrip when you took the power from the transporter into yourself."

I frowned. "Should I be worried I might fall to pieces in a couple of days?"

"I don't think so," he said. "It takes a life to save one, and you killed at least one spirit mage during the fight, didn't you?"

My mouth parted. "I'm really glad the Crow didn't figure out that one."

He'd come close, though. Close enough for me to suspect the curse had always had a secret clause hidden within it. Had the Order done that on purpose, or was it simply that they'd hoped no spirit mages would ever survive for long enough to work it out?

The transporter lit up and the Elemental Soldiers appeared on the platform, except for Bria. Now I thought back, she hadn't been in the other citadel, either.

"What in hell happened?" Ryan said. "You both disappeared, and then came back with—who was that guy with Hawker?"

"Dirk Alban." Elements, I was tired. "You know what the enemy took from the vampires? Turns out they had a soul amulet hidden somewhere."

"Who…" Felicity broke off, staring at Greyson. "The *Death King?* You're alive?"

Even though he regularly used an illusion to appear human, it was obvious this wasn't the same. He was breathing hard, and bruising spread up one side of his stunned face.

"Don't get too excited," said Greyson. "The cantrip that brought me back to life has deactivated. Nobody else can use it."

"Any cursed cantrip can be used in the same way, though," I told the others. "The machines are like batteries for cantrips, except they're powered by the life force of living beings. I don't know how long the lives sacrificed in London will keep the transporter in Elysium linked up to that new node, but we need to shut it down. I reckon one of Devon's neutralising cantrips will do the trick."

"Way ahead of you," said Ryan. "But seriously, did you say *Dirk Alban* was back? He left you here and didn't take you with him?"

"I turned him down," I said, unable to stop the grin from sweeping across my face.

Sure, I knew there'd be hell to pay later, but I was alive, while Greyson was living and breathing once again.

If that wasn't a victory, I didn't know what was.

24

I rolled the die and whooped. "Natural twenty. Thank you, lucky dice."

Our weekly D&D game was in full swing, and this time I was a full participant. Devon was thrilled to have me back, as were the others, though I had yet to give everyone an explanation of how I'd pulled it off. I still didn't know how to deal with the implications that the spirit mages' life force could return the dead to life… or that the Parallel might well have been built on the back of lives sacrificed in the same way.

Once Greyson and I had left the citadel, Ryan had taken Devon's neutralising cantrips to shut down the transporter linking the citadel to the new node in London. It might not be a permanent solution, but I'd rest easier knowing Dirk Alban and Hawker wouldn't be able to set their armies loose on the city.

"And the evil lich lord is no more." Devon knocked over the miniature with a flick of her finger. "Nice job, crew."

Trix and I high-fived each other across the table, while Dex flew around our heads.

"Nice." He circled the table, halting above Devon's head. "Say, you don't have an illusion cantrip which works on sprites? I wouldn't mind rolling a die myself."

"No," said Devon. "Besides, I'd get swamped by the other sprites asking for one, too."

"You aren't wrong." New sprites showed up at the castle every week, drawn to Dex's open offer to let anyone join his squad, as the others we'd freed from the citadel had scattered throughout the Parallel. Greyson didn't seem to mind them coming to the castle, but he hadn't put an official statement out on anything after his return from death nearly a week ago. The only person he'd called to speak with him had been Bria of all people, and she'd refused to tell anyone what he'd said in their meeting.

Speaking of Bria, she sat on the opposite side of the table, our newest group member. Dex, for reasons I couldn't fathom, had insisted on inviting her to join our campaign, and the others had warmed to her faster than I'd expected. While it hadn't escaped my attention that she'd vanished at some point during the battle, Dex insisted she'd helped both Trix and Ryan drive off the remainder of Hawker's allies and ensured the transporter stayed deactivated for as long as possible. She was entitled to keep her secrets, so I let it slide. For now.

On the other side of the table, Trix and Ryan sat close to one another. I hadn't yet asked if they'd had an honest discussion of their feelings, though we'd all been run off our feet lately as a result of the lich lord's real-life counterpart taking an inexplicable sabbatical.

We took a break from the game for five minutes to

order takeout, and I seized the opportunity to ask Ryan about our missing lich lord.

"I haven't spoken to him," they said. "Well, he did come out of his room yesterday, but it was just to ask if anyone else had left the castle. I think he assumes his liches are going to leave in droves now he isn't immortal."

"That's ridiculous," I said. "I'll go and talk to him. Maybe I can help."

What was going on with him? Okay, I was thrilled to be alive, but he might not be. Supposedly, he'd sequestered himself in the castle to deal with the side effects of his abrupt return to the land of the living and hadn't even been sending his Elemental Soldiers out on missions, but now was not the best time for him to inconveniently vanish.

"Is this a bad time to tell you the Order is in the papers again?" said Trix. "The magical world's papers, I mean."

"Damn," I said. "No, but there's never a good time for the Order."

"I concur," said Devon. "Go on, get it over with."

Trix handed me a folded-up paper. I looked at the front page and anger clenched my hands. "They're blaming *Greyson* for the deaths in London?"

"Not just him," said Trix. "They're blaming your Spirit Agent friends, too."

"Dickheads." I sat back down, a leaden feeling descending on me. The Order hadn't said a word to us since the battle, but Mr Holland would be pissed at me for slithering out of his grasp, and Hawker would have told them I was responsible for wrecking his and Alban's plans. Maybe Alban would vouch for me, but who knew. It still eluded me what his endgame was, though I assumed his plans hadn't included being stuck in an amulet for a decade. In any case, the battle might be over, but the node in the middle of London remained intact, while dormant, and I had little doubt the enemy would try to use it again.

My phone buzzed with a call. I checked the number. Mum. "Let me take this."

"Come back when the game starts again," Devon called after me.

I left the room, phone in hand. "Hey, Mum."

"Oh, good," she said. "I was starting to worry."

"Yeah, I've had a lot going on," I said. "Sorry. How's Elise?"

"She's great!" she said in enthusiastic tones.

We chatted for a few minutes until the doorbell rang. Our takeout had arrived.

"I have to get back to the game," I said, "but I'll see you later."

"You're back, then?" she asked.

She couldn't possibly know how deeply her words hit me, but emotion choked me as I responded. "I'm back for the long haul, if I have anything to do with it. Promise."

———

The next morning, I walked through the node and entered the Court of the Dead. I hadn't had an official invitation, but it was about time Greyson addressed the liches before they did leave him for Hawker and Alban after all. I understood why he might have reservations, but his people wanted answers, and the Elemental Soldiers did, too. Who could blame them?

When I walked towards the castle, I spotted Bria chatting to some of the Spirit Agents. She was the only person who'd actually spoken to the Death King since the battle and she refused to share what they'd discussed, but at this point, I was all but certain she was on our side. Sure, she had secrets, but who didn't?

"Seen the Death King?" I asked her.

"Nope," she said. "Are you here to drag him out?"

"I hope dragging won't be necessary, but yes," I said. "What've you been doing since the battle?"

"We've been patrolling the wasteland around the citadel," she said. "And trying to find where Hawker ran off to, but no matter how many times we use the transporter in Arcadia, we can't reach it. I think maybe only you and the Death King can."

"I'll tell him." It was risky for us to leave the transporter in Arcadia active, but Devon could only make so many neutralising cantrips at a time and we needed to have one route by which to track down the enemy.

I looked past Bria, seeing someone else lurking outside the gates. Lord Blackbourne. I'd wondered when he'd show his face again.

"Looking for the Death King?" I strode over to him. "I'm on my way to see him right now. I'll tell him you're here."

"Do that," he said. "I've had considerable trouble getting hold of him."

"I'm glad you're here to explain why you had Dirk Alban's soul in your basement," I added. "I expect a reasonable explanation."

Without waiting for a response, I climbed the steps to the castle. Greyson wasn't in the entrance hall. He wasn't in the hall of souls, either. That left one place, so I walked through the door at the back right of the hall, climbed the stairs to his private suite, and knocked on the door.

Greyson answered a moment later, dressed in a dark pair of trousers and a shirt, with his hair slightly damp like he'd just showered. For the first time in a while, probably. His features were softer, more human. More like the boy from my memories. He'd hung his armoured coat over the back of a chair, a pair of heavy-looking dark boots next to it. I was pretty sure he'd rearranged the furniture, too. I bit back an unexpected laugh at the notion that the first thing the Death King had wanted to do upon his return to life was to redecorate the place.

"What is it?" he said. Even his voice sounded different, less cold. I couldn't believe it'd taken so long for me to realise it was him I'd heard in my memories of Dirk Alban's death.

"Greyson, everyone is looking for you," I said to him.

"Like who?" he said.

"Lord Blackbourne, for one," I said. "The other Elemental Soldiers, too. I think they're waiting for you to give them orders."

"Are you sure they're not just waiting for me to abdicate?"

"What?" I blinked. "No. Unless you're planning on staying in your room forever."

He gave a short laugh. "I have no idea how to tell the others I had no intention of being the first person to be cured of the curse without inviting every lich in the castle to strike me down on the spot."

"You're scared of your own people?" I said incredulously. "Really, Greyson. They're not going to have you killed just because you found the cure they've been looking for over the last thirty-odd years."

"I'm not scared of them," he said. "I'm concerned about what this means for our Court. They need someone strong in charge."

"Strong doesn't mean immortal," I argued. "I didn't get to be immortal for long, but I don't think I was any stronger as a lich than I am now."

"You're a hundred times stronger than I'll ever be." He leaned against the sofa and tugged on one of his knee-high boots, his fingers fumbling the buckles. "I can barely even button my coat, let alone defend a Court of several hundred liches from an oncoming army."

"You were dead for ten years," I said. "If it's any consolation, Dirk Alban is probably having the same difficulty."

He grabbed the other boot. "I keep expecting him to walk in here and try to claim dominion over the Court of the Dead. Technically, he bested the last Death King, so the law would work in his favour."

"He won't be very popular among the other liches," I said. "Look, Greyson—chill. Nobody is going to usurp you. Even if they try, the Elemental Soldiers will stand behind you. And I will, too."

He looked at me for a moment, a lock of dark hair falling into his eyes. I suppressed the urge to push it aside. "I appreciate your loyalty, but not everyone is the same."

"It's not just loyalty," I said. "You've led this place since you were what, eighteen? I'm pretty sure you weren't always certain of your decisions. Being human amplifies all your uncertainties, I know, but you're still the same person you were before. If the liches can't recognise that, it's their problem, not yours."

He grabbed his armoured coat, shrugging into it. "I feel like this is better designed for a lich than for a human."

"Looks fine to me." Better than fine. While he'd lost a few inches of height now his feet were planted firmly on the ground, the armoured coat brought back the intimidating factor and he looked almost like the old Death King by the time he straightened upright. "You just need a mask if you want to hide your face. You can carry a big sword around now, too."

He smoothed his hair down. "I seriously doubt the liches will find that impressive."

I snorted. "Don't forget Lord Blackbourne is outside. Imagine the look on his face if you come out waving a medieval weapon in his face. Considering he lied about keeping Dirk Alban's soul in his basement, it'd serve him right."

He frowned. "He can drain my blood now. That's not something I foresaw."

"I bet he'll start grovelling to you instead," I said. "Did his people raise a hand to help you in the battle?"

"No." His expression shuttered. "They didn't. Let's see to him."

He walked out of the room and closed the door behind him, while I hurried to catch up. Downstairs, we crossed the entrance hall and found the vampire waiting outside the doors.

Lord Blackbourne made a big show of checking his watch. "There you are, Greyson."

"What do you want with me, Lord Blackbourne?" said Greyson.

"Lost your manners as well as your immortality?" said the vampire.

"Lord Blackbourne," I said warningly. Maybe this had been a mistake. "Are you going to explain what Dirk Alban's soul amulet was doing in your house?"

"It was dormant," he said. "No matter what we did, we were unable to destroy it. I thought nobody knew its location."

"I'm guessing someone at the Order must have," I said. "Someone who told Hawker. Perhaps they knew you were the one who stole the video of my trial, so they figured that wasn't all you stole."

He scowled. "What's done is done. My people will be leaving Arcadia in the days to come, regardless."

"You're going into hiding?" I said, incredulous. "There are people who need you."

"I have to disagree," he said. "My fellow vampires need me more than the city does. Also, that fire mage of yours was asking for you."

"He isn't mine," I said, conscious of Greyson's eyes on me. "What did Brant want?"

"He was concerned you would meet a deadly end after your return to life, given that cursed cantrip." His gaze slid between us. "You both appear to be fine."

"That's because we figured out how it works," I said. "Those cursed cantrips *can* return someone to life, if they're combined with a strong enough energy source. It's the same with the Crow's other cantrips, I don't doubt."

"As well as the transporters in the citadels," added Greyson. "Which we haven't found a permanent way to shut down yet. Is that why you're running away?"

"Wouldn't you do the same?" said Lord Blackbourne.

"No," said Greyson. "If you have no intention of offering your assistance, then I will gladly step in to take leadership of Arcadia in your absence."

"Huh?" I said. Whatever happened to abdicating? Apparently, he'd decided to go to the opposite extreme. I knew adjusting to being human again was a hell of a shakeup, but I hadn't a clue what was going through his head at the moment.

"That won't be necessary," said Lord Blackbourne. "The city can take care of itself."

"I beg to differ," said Greyson. "Besides, if you're leaving, it shouldn't matter."

The vampire shifted on his feet. "Now wait just one minute—"

Ah. Now I understood what Greyson was doing—goading the vampire into staying in Arcadia. As the two of them broke into an argument, I scanned the grounds, spotting several liches approach their leader from a distance. I wasn't sure he'd even given them an update on the status of Hawker, let alone told them Alban was alive again.

Dirk Alban hadn't been seen since the battle. Nor had Hawker, though I had little doubt that he and his allies were working hard to establish their control over the Order. At some point, they'd come for the Court of the Dead, too. Which meant we had to be ready.

Lord Blackbourne noticed the liches approaching, too. "Fine, then. I will discuss our options with my fellow vampires. Good day."

He departed, while I arched a brow at Greyson. "Is he considering sticking around?"

"Yes, but I believe he'll be moving his headquarters away from the citadel," he said. "Long overdue, really."

"I think your liches want to hear from you." I looked him in the eyes. "Go on. It'll be fine. You owe them."

"I do owe them." He raised his voice and addressed the liches drifting around the grounds. "Come to the entrance hall, all of you. I will speak to you there."

The liches approached the castle doors. I walked up the steps ahead of him and opened the door so we could walk through it while the liches glided straight through the wood. I heard whispers among them, but nobody moved to attack us. So far, so good.

Greyson strode towards the dais, and the liches gathered to listen to him. I positioned myself on the front row, a sense of pride rising inside me. He held his head high, same as usual, but without the mask of a lich to hide his features or disguise the fact that he was as living and breathing as I was.

"I apologise for my absence," said Greyson, when the last of the liches fell into place. "And for returning to life with no explanation."

A long, disgruntled mutter travelled among the liches.

"Most of you won't remember the House of Spirit as it once was," he went on, "but we lived like this before the war, and I will do everything in my power to ensure you are removed from the curse's effects, too."

"You promised to let us be saved first," said one of the liches. "Why did you go back on your word?"

"Because I made him do it." I walked out in front of them and climbed onto the dais. "Hawker attacked him with a cantrip which would have killed him, but I saved his life. Dead or alive, you need a leader who cares about you like Greyson does. To save all of you would have required sacrificing many innocent lives, and we couldn't do that."

Greyson gave a nod, his expression showing hints of both surprise and gratitude. "Olivia is right. The fact remains that we face a foe unlike any other. Dirk Alban lives, and he and Hawker have taken over London's branches of the Order of the Elements."

He gave the liches a short explanation of the events of the battle, as well as an addition about the vampires' decision to remain in Arcadia for now. The liches didn't appear thrilled at his explanation of the revival of the citadels and the unclear elements in how he'd come back to life, but none of them shouted an objection or tried to attack either of us, so I called that a win.

When he'd finished addressing the liches, they dispersed, while the Elemental Soldiers stayed behind in the hall. He then gave them a few orders, and they left. Then Greyson and I were alone together. Cold air blew through the main hall, and I shivered.

"Now you'll understand why we kept complaining about how cold it was in here," I said to him.

"It's not that bad," he said. "Don't forget I grew up around spirit mages."

"What happened to your soul amulet?" I asked.

"It's empty," he said. "Dormant. Theoretically, I could reuse it if I became a lich again. There's some power left inside it, but not my soul. Life essence might be finite, but it can be replenished. Want to see it?"

"Sure." I walked with him through to the hall of souls, and a blast of icy air swept over us when he opened the door.

Greyson led the way over to a shelf where his soul amulet lay beside mine. Two identical disc-like shapes covered in runes, each imprinted with the image of a skull etched into the metal surface. Not so much as a wisp of energy remained inside them, no signs that they'd once held the fragile essence of our souls. I still marvelled that someone as strong as a lich had to depend on something so ephemeral.

"You can take yours home with you if you like," he said.

"Nah, leave it there." My heartbeat sounded unusually loud in the wide, empty hall. "Are your powers still intact? Your spirit magic, I mean?"

"Of course," he said. "As far as I'm aware."

"We can still use the nodes, too," I said. "There's nothing you could do as a lich which you can't do now. Except go all shadowy and terrify everyone."

"Never underestimate the impact of being able to go all shadowy and terrify everyone when you rule a kingdom of liches."

I laughed, the sound echoing off the high ceiling. "Maybe, but there are other perks to being human. You won't fall to pieces if you visit Earth anymore, for one thing."

"What else?"

"And you can join in game night," I said. "Roll a die."

"I heard you did a decent job of that even as a lich."

"Not playing video games, I didn't," I said. "I kept dropping the controller. You can't say you didn't miss anything about being human?"

"Some things," he said. "Truth be told, I forgot most of them."

"That's okay." I faced Greyson and drew in a breath. "I'm not going to turn around and find you've severed your soul again, am I?"

"No," he said. "Mostly because I'm not sure the cure can be repeated. If I turn into a lich again, I might not be able to turn back. Especially if it comes with such a heavy cost."

"Yeah," I said. "Understandable. I just wanted you to know, though… I kinda like you like this."

"You do?" he said.

"Sure." I looked him up and down to better appreciate the view of the solid, warm presence in place of the cold king of the liches. Then I slipped my hand up his jaw, marvelled at how soft his hair was, and drew his head down on mine. He sighed against my mouth, and I deepened the kiss. The feel of his heartbeat racing against my fingers gave me a thrill, as did the brightness in his eyes as he looked down at me.

"Are you sure you want this?" he said. "As a lich, I was so successful at adapting to death that I forgot much of what it means to be human. I'm not so sure I can be the man I once was."

"And I'm still missing a chunk of my memories," I said. "We'll be fine. You'll just have to remind me of everything we did the first time around."

"Or we could make new memories," he said. "This is a second life for me as well as you."

"Now we're talking." I smiled up at him. "C'mon, let's go see the other Elemental Soldiers. Maybe I'll give you an invite to our next games night."

"Should I be worried?" he said. "I recall overhearing something about an evil lich lord."

Oops. "You heard?"

"I imagine you hoped I wouldn't." A smile tugged his lips upward. "I'm flattered to have been immortalised in your game."

"Don't get too excited. We killed him with my lucky dice during the last campaign." I caught his arm and walked with him out of the hall of souls. "Can't have it all."

The castle beckoned to us, as well as the world beyond. Could we make it work? Two former liches, strangers and old friends all at once?

I didn't know, but I was willing to give it a try.

ABOUT THE AUTHOR

Emma is the New York Times and USA Today Bestselling author of the Changeling Chronicles urban fantasy series.

Emma spent her childhood creating imaginary worlds to compensate for a disappointingly average reality, so it was probably inevitable that she ended up writing fantasy novels. When she's not immersed in her own fictional universes, Emma can be found with her head in a book or wandering around the world in search of adventure.

Find out more about Emma's books at
www.emmaladams.com.